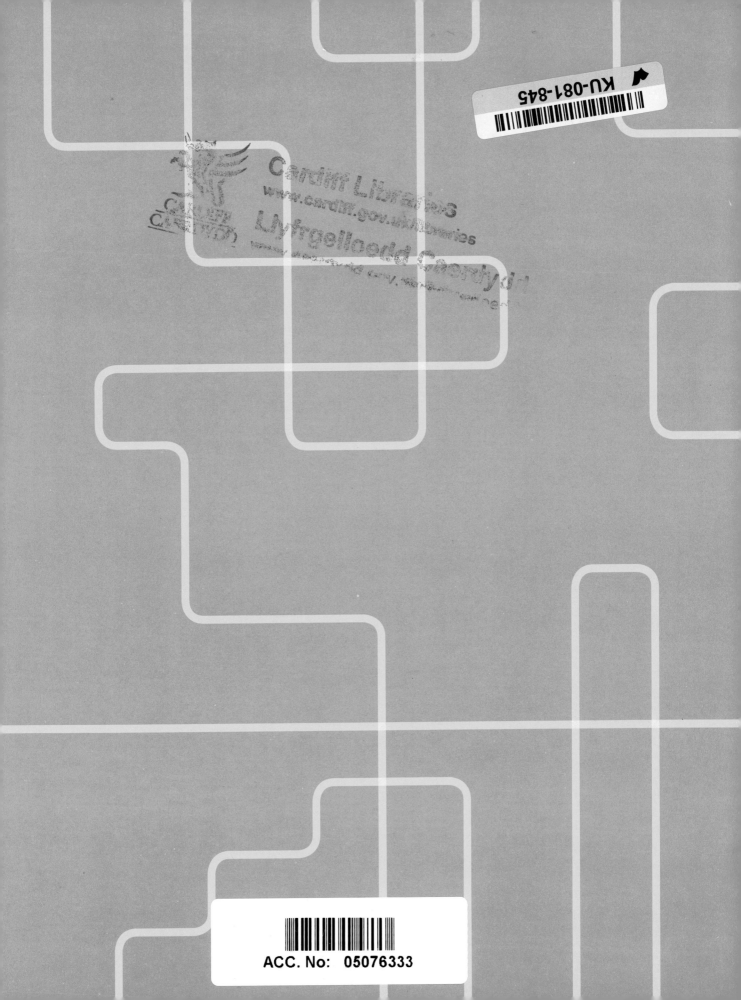

HABITATS

ANNA CLAYBOURNE

W
FRANKLIN WATTS
LONDON•SYDNEY

Franklin Watts
First published in Great Britain in 2017 by The Watts Publishing Group

Credits
Series Editor: Amy Pimperton
Series Designer: Emma DeBanks
Picture Researcher: Diana Morris

Picture credits: aabeele/Shutterstock: 15b. Franco Banfi/Nature PL: 11b. Randy Beacham/Alamy: 23t. Hagit Berkovich/
Shutterstock: 16t. BlueRingMedia/Shutterstock: 9b. Aleksandr Bryliaev/Shutterstock: 27cl. Rich Carey/Shutterstock: front cover,
24t. Patricia Chumillas/Shutterstock: 13c. Paul Crash/Shutterstock: 3bc. Designua/Shutterstock: 5t. Domnitsky/Shutterstock:
21t. Dorling Kindersely/Getty Images: 24b. ecliptic blue/Shutterstock: 22tr. Armando Frazão/Dreamstime: 8b. Eric Gevaert/
Dreamstime: 26t. Volodymyr Goinyk/Shutterstock: 3br. GooDween123/Shutterstock: 8tr. greboha/Shutterstock: 12t, 29b. Vitalij
Gumenuk/Dreamstime: 10b. Image source/Alamy: 11c. Eric Isselee/Shutterstock: 11t, 29t. Ivto/Shutterstock: 14b. Natalie Jean/
Shutterstock: 18br. Alain Dragesco-Joffe/Biofoto/FLPA: 5b. Jukhu/Shutterstock: 21b. Julia/Shutterstock: 27t. Dmitry Kalinovsky/
Shutterstock: 20t. Nancy Kennedy/Dreamstime: 1, 18t. Kichigin/Shutterstock: 12c, 12b. Phillip Kinsey/Dreamstime: 13t. Kateryna
Kon/Shutterstock: 8cr. Kurzon/CC Wikimedia Commons: 16b. kzww/Shutterstock: 19b. Mike Lane45/Dreamstime: 4tr. Mihai
Bogdan Lazar/Dreamstime: 16c. Libra/Shutterstock: 27cr. Michael Ludwig/Dreamstime: 6b. Lukaves/Dreamstime: 10c. Bruce
Macqueen/Dreamstime: 20c. Robert McGouey/Wildlife/Alamy: 25t. Mirage 3/Dreamstime: 17b. Sergei Mironenko/Shutterstock:
8cl. Moravska/Shutterstock: 22tl. Nature Diver/Shutterstock: 18bc. PRILL/Shutterstock: 6c. Menno Schaefe/Shutterstock: 18bl.
Scubaluna/Shutterstock: 24c. Guillermo Guerao Serra/Shutterstock: 15t. Andrei Shumskiy/Shutterstock: 7r. Snova/Shutterstock: 26b.
Kenneth Sponsier/Shutterstock: 26c. Stockconnection/Superstock: 23b. Studiotouch/Shutterstock: 22tc. USFWS/Alamy: 6t. Varuna/
Shutterstock: 27c. Vaclav Volrab/Dreamstime: 7b. Piotr Wawryzyniuk/Shutterstock: 14c. Steve Winter/Getty
Images: 14t. Paul Wolf/Dreamstime: 4bl. Rudmer Zwerver/Dreamstime: 13b.

HB ISBN 978 1 4451 5147 2
PB ISBN 978 1 4451 5148 9

Printed in China

Franklin Watts
An imprint of
Hachette Children's Group
Part of The Watts Publishing Group
Carmelite House
50 Victoria Embankment
London EC4Y 0DZ

An Hachette UK Company
www.hachette.co.uk

www.franklinwatts.co.uk

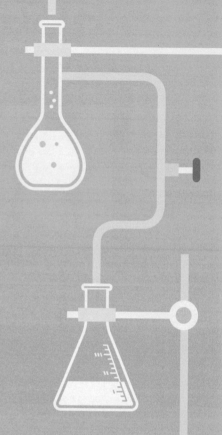

CONTENTS

What is a habitat? 4

The science of habitats 6

Working scientifically 7

Wildlife habitats 8

Adaptations 10

Moving in... 12

Blending in 14

Extreme habitats 16

Keystone species.. 18

How trees help.. 20

Balancing the numbers 22

Building the environment 24

Climate change 26

Reading your results... 28

Glossary.. 30

Books and websites... 31

Index 32

Worlds in **bold** can be found in the glossary on page 30.

WHAT IS A HABITAT?

A habitat is the natural home of an animal, plant or other living thing. Each type, or **species**, of living thing has its own habitat, where it is found in the wild.

For example, the sand cat is a desert animal. Its natural habitat is sandy or rocky deserts in North Africa and parts of Asia.

Living things are **adapted**, or suited, to their habitats. The sand cat has fur on the soles of its feet to help it walk over hot sand. Its fur also keeps it warm at night, when deserts can be cold. Its big ears and sharp eyesight help it find small prey in the dark.

A sand cat prowls around its natural habitat, a sandy desert.

A humpback whale roams its home, the open ocean.

THE RIGHT HABITAT

Each living thing, or **organism**, needs to be in the right habitat to survive. Put the sand cat in the North Atlantic Ocean and it would not be happy! It wouldn't be able to swim for long, or hold its breath underwater to go hunting. Its thick fur would get wet and become heavy, and it would soon get too cold.

On the other hand, a humpback whale is adapted to life in the ocean, with its flippers, rubbery skin, and a blowhole on its head for breathing. But in the desert it wouldn't survive a day. It would overheat and be unable to move.

This means that if habitats change or get damaged, living things can struggle to survive. For example, forest creatures, such as monkeys, can die if their forest habitat is cut down.

HABITATS AND BIOMES

A habitat can be big, like a desert, or small like a pond or an old, hollow log. On a large scale, the Earth's surface can be divided into several main habitat types, called **biomes**. Each biome also contains many smaller habitats.

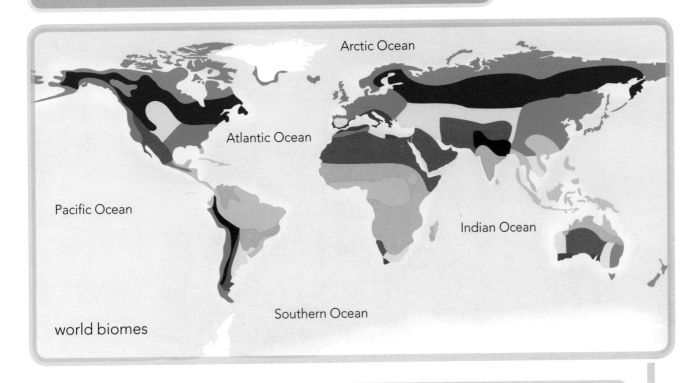

Arctic Ocean

Atlantic Ocean

Pacific Ocean

Indian Ocean

Southern Ocean

world biomes

- tropical rainforest
- northern forest
- **deciduous** forest
- **tundra**

- tropical **savanna**
- temperate grassland
- Mediterranean vegetation
- desert

- seas and oceans
- ice sheet and polar desert
- mountains

ECOSYSTEMS

An **ecosystem** means a habitat and all the things living in it. Besides needing the right habitat, living things depend on other organisms in their ecosystem. For example, a sand cat needs desert rodents and lizards to feed on. In turn, these animals need to eat desert plants or insects.

Sand cats hunt and eat **venomous** snakes.

THE SCIENCE OF HABITATS

The word science means 'knowledge'. Throughout history, humans have experimented with all kinds of things in order to learn more about the world. That's partly because we have a natural urge to find things out.

Scientists use viewers to observe plants and animals in a river habitat.

Studying and understanding habitats is especially important – not just for its own sake, but for other reasons too.

Many living things are **endangered**, or at risk of dying out and becoming **extinct**. That's partly because of changes humans have made to the world, such as clearing wild forests for cities or farmland.

Climate change affects habitats. It can make them warmer, colder, wetter or drier than they should be. This can cause problems for the organisms that live there.

The more scientists know about how processes such as climate change work, the more we can help endangered animals to survive, and protect and preserve natural surroundings.

The forest on the right of this picture is being cut down to make room for farmland.

Some types of coral struggle to survive in oceans warmed by climate change.

HUMAN HABITAT

Humans are living things too, and the whole world is our ecosystem. We depend on other living things for our survival. Protecting habitats and ecosystems not only helps them, but also helps us.

WORKING SCIENTIFICALLY

In this book, you'll find a range of investigations or experiments that will help you discover how habitats and ecosystems work.

To do experiments, scientists use careful, logical methods to make sure they get reliable results. The experiments and investigations in this book use four key scientific methods, along with an easy acronym to help you remember them: **ATOM**.

ASK

What do you want to find out?

Asking questions is a really important part of science. Scientists think about what questions they want to answer, and how to do that.

TEST

Setting up an experiment that will test ideas and answer questions

Scientists then design experiments to answer their questions. A test works best if you only test for one thing at a time.

OBSERVE

Key things to look out for

Scientists watch their experiments closely to see what is happening.

MEASURE

Measuring and recording results, such as temperatures, sizes or amounts of time

Making accurate measurements and recording the results shows what the experiment has revealed.

WHAT NEXT?

After each experiment, the 'What next?' section gives you ideas for more activities and experiments, or ways to display your results.

WILDLIFE HABITATS

Wherever you live, even if it's a town or city, there will be habitats where living things are found. Habitats near you might include gardens, hedgerows, woods, moorland, the seashore or a local park.

Untidy, overgrown gardens make a great habitat for insects, birds and snails.

HOME HABITATS

Our own homes are habitats, too. Some living things, such as houseflies, silverfish, moulds and house spiders are well-suited to living alongside us. What types of creepy-crawlies have you seen sharing your home? In fact, the human body is also a habitat! Many types of **bacteria** live on our skin and inside our bodies. Some bacteria can make you ill, but most are harmless.

Silverfish aren't fish, but fish-shaped insects. They like living in damp cellars or bathrooms.

actual size

Bacteria in our intestines help us to digest food, and to keep other, more harmful bacteria away.

Notepad
Pen or pencil
Optional:
Magnifying glass
or bug viewer
Camera or smartphone
Binoculars

SCIENCE EXPERIMENT:

HABITAT TRAIL

Choose a local habitat that you can reach easily, such as a garden at home or school, or a park, and go wildlife spotting.

Always be careful around water, and make sure an adult is with you.

 Ask

What kinds of wildlife do you think you'll find in this habitat?

 Test

- Look for living things in the habitat — including animals, such as insects and birds, plants like flowers and trees, and things like moulds, **fungi**, algae and lichens.
- Use any gear you have, such as a magnifying glass or binoculars, to look more closely.

Observe

How do the living things behave, and how do they suit their habitat? Can you see anything eating anything else, and if so, who was eating what? Write down each thing you find, and take photographs if possible.

 Measure

How many of each type of thing can you see? For example, how many insects, birds, flowers or lichens?

WHAT NEXT?

Write up a report on your habitat and the types of living things you found in it. Think about what season it is — do you think this affects what you might have seen? You could even make a map showing where you spotted each thing.

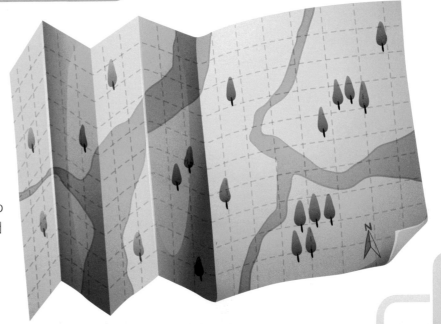

ADAPTATIONS

Living things are adapted to their habitats, meaning they are well-suited to them. Each living thing has body parts, and ways of behaving, moving and feeding that fit well with its habitat.

EVOLVING AND CHANGING

Adaptation happens over a long time, thanks to a process called **evolution**. In each species, or type of living thing, some individuals are better-suited to their habitats than others. For example, they may have better **camouflage**. These better-suited individuals tend to live longer and have more babies, and pass on these features to their young. In this way, over many **generations**, species change to adapt to their surroundings. For example, reptiles evolved from fish over millions of years. They adapted from a watery habitat to a land habitat.

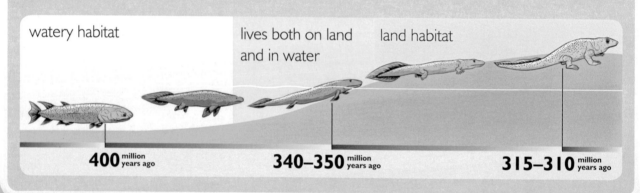

watery habitat

lives both on land and in water

land habitat

400 million years ago

340–350 million years ago

315–310 million years ago

This caterpillar is camouflaged to look like a twig.

SCIENCE EXPERIMENT:

POND DIPPING

If there's a pond or rock pool you can visit, you can observe the living things that live there, such as a water boatman (right), to see how they are adapted to their habitat.

Always be careful around water, and make sure an adult is with you.

actual size

Ask

How are living things in a pond or rock pool adapted to a water habitat?

Test

- Look for living things in and under the water, floating on it, moving on it or moving over it.
- Collect water samples in your containers, and see if there are creatures in the water when you look closely, or with a magnifying glass.
- You can also use clear plastic containers as underwater viewers by half-submerging them in the water.

Observe

Look for the features that help each living thing survive in the water. Do they swim or move in other ways? What features or parts do they have that help them swim, float, skate or dive?

Measure

Which animal moves the fastest? Which living thing is the most common in the pond or pool?

WHAT NEXT?

Think about sea creatures, such as sharks, whales, sea snakes or giant squid. What adaptations do they have to their habitat?

A magnifying glass will help you spot tiny water animals.

How do a giant squid's large eyes help it adapt to its **environment**?

MOVING IN

When a habitat exists, with the food and surroundings that living things need, those living things will move in and take advantage of it. This is especially true of moulds!

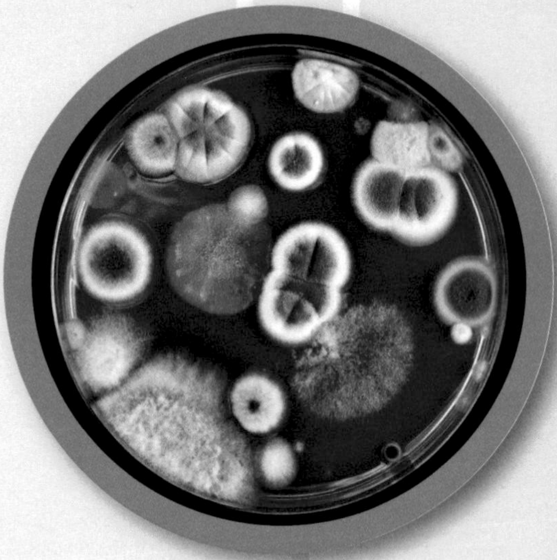

GOING MOULDY

Moulds are a type of fungus, and are related to mushrooms and toadstools. Fungi are not plants or animals, but a separate family of living things. They feed on soil, plants or animals through a network of tiny thread-like roots, called a **mycelium**.

A fungus grows stalks or other shapes, called **fruiting bodies**, which release spores. Spores are like tiny seeds. They drift around in the air and settle on surfaces. If they land somewhere with a good food supply, they start to grow.

To study moulds, scientists grow them in **Petri dishes**.

A puffball fungus releases millions of spores in a puffy cloud.

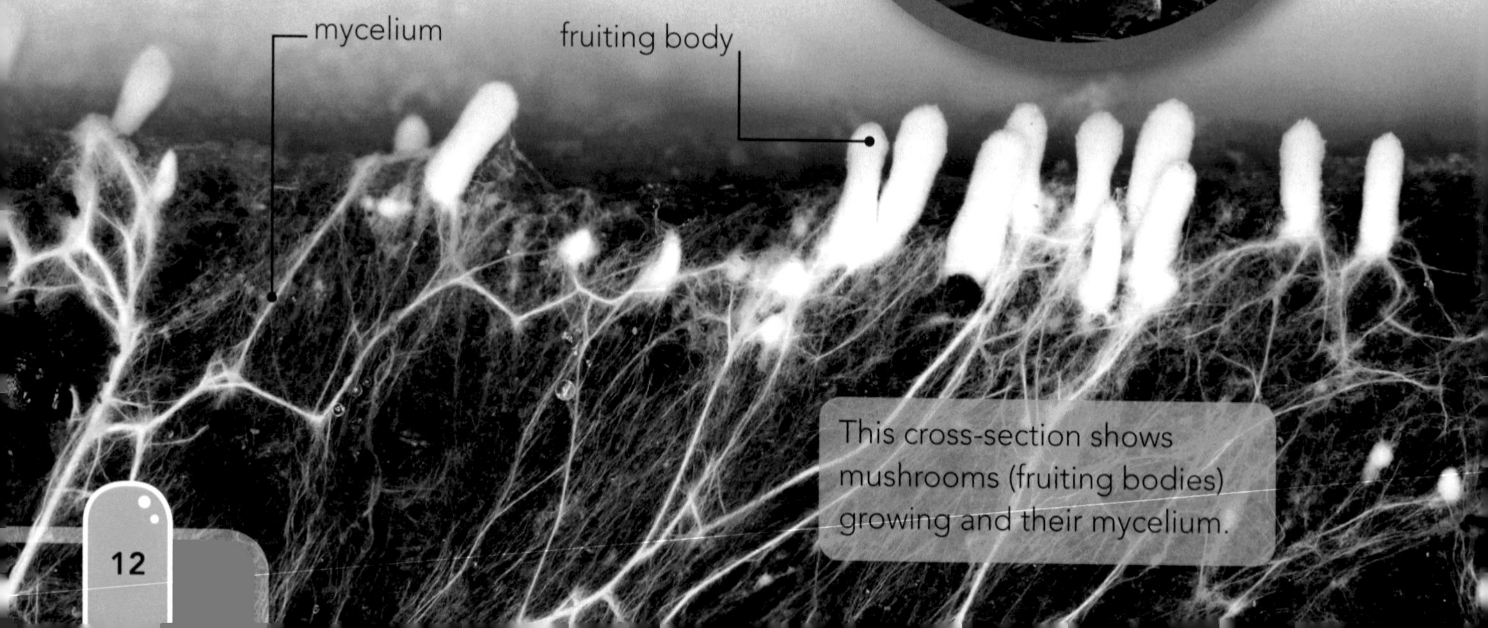

mycelium

fruiting body

This cross-section shows mushrooms (fruiting bodies) growing and their mycelium.

12

SCIENCE EXPERIMENT:
MOULD GARDEN

Create a habitat for moulds, and watch to see what grows.

Moulds can be bad for you, so don't open the mould garden. After the experiment, throw the whole thing away.

YOU WILL NEED:

Clear, disposable jar or container with lid
Old leftover food
Water
Sticky tape

 ASK

If you make a nice welcoming habitat for moulds, which ones will move in? Which foods do different moulds prefer?

 TEST

- Collect some pieces of old, leftover bread, cake, cheese, fruit and/or vegetables.
- Put a chunk of each food in your container and leave it open for a few hours.
- Add a few drops of water, then put the lid on tightly and seal closed with sticky tape.
- Leave the mould garden at room temperature for about five days.

 OBSERVE

Each day, take a good look at your mould garden to see if anything is growing.

 MEASURE

How many different types of mould have grown? How fast do they grow? What food does each mould prefer?

WHAT NEXT?

If you have a garden, try making another habitat by leaving one corner to go wild. Then check to see what plant and animal wildlife moves in.

A variety of moulds grow on rotting fruit.

You might spot a common shrew in the undergrowth in a wild garden.

BLENDING IN

Camouflage helps living things by making them harder to see within their habitat. Their markings or shapes blend in with the background, making them seem almost invisible.

HUNTING AND ESCAPING

Camouflage is useful for both **predators** (hunters) and **prey** (animals that get eaten). Predators can hide while sneaking up on their prey. Prey can hide to avoid being caught and eaten. For it to work, though, they have to match the habitat they live in very closely.

A flounder (a type of fish) has camouflage that helps it hide on the seabed to avoid being eaten.

A tiger's stripes help it to 'disappear' among long grasses as it stalks its prey.

Can you see the flounder hiding here?

PLANT CAMOUFLAGE

There are even plants that have camouflage. Pebble plants are desert plants that look like stones, putting animals off eating them.

A pebble plant grows among real stones in a desert.

CREATING CAMOUFLAGE

Design your own camouflaged creatures to see if you can trick your friends. Can you create camouflage as convincing as it is in real life, such as the camouflage of the yellow crab spider hiding in the flower (above, right)?

YOU WILL NEED:

A computer,
Internet connection
and printer
Paper
Scissors
Coloured pens and pencils

ASK

How can you create creatures that are really well-camouflaged in different environments?

TEST

- Search online for photos of habitats, such as a leafy forest, sandy desert or a colourful coral reef.
- Print out a few of the clearest, most detailed pictures.
- On your paper, design some living things (such as insects, lizards or fish) that will be well-camouflaged in these habitats. (You can copy these shapes or draw your own.)

OBSERVE

Cut out your designs and place them on their backgrounds so that they are well hidden. Give a friend or classmate ten seconds to see how many of your creatures they can spot.

MEASURE

Count the number that were spotted. Did any of your creations escape being found? These creatures would be the best at surviving in real life.

WHAT NEXT?

Humans use camouflage too. Can you think of ways we do this, and what our camouflage looks like?

Why do you think this photographer is wearing camouflage?

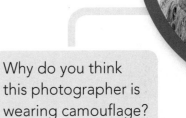

EXTREME HABITATS

Even extremely harsh habitats, like the Antarctic and high mountains, have ecosystems. They are home to living things that are adapted to survive there, and have evolved special features that help them to endure the extremes.

Besides being used for hearing, the fennec fox's big ears help heat escape from its body in the Sahara Desert.

The plant, edelweiss, grows high-up on mountains. It has thick fur to protect it from the cold.

BLUBBER

Animals that swim in cold water, such as seals, whales and polar bears, often have a thick layer of fat under their skin, called **blubber**. The blubber acts like a blanket, helping the important organs inside their bodies to stay warm.

blubber

This view inside a whale shows its layer of blubber under its skin.

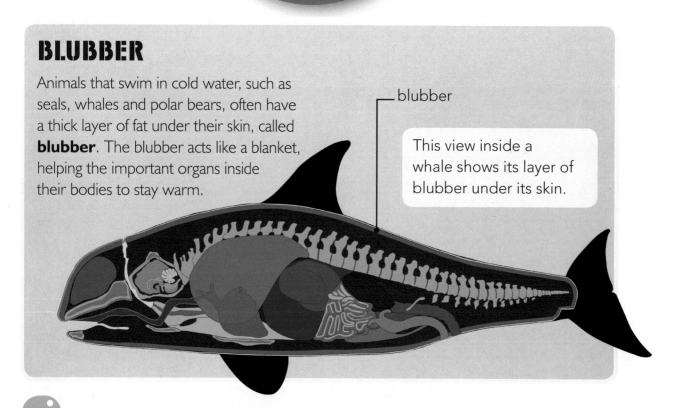

SCIENCE EXPERIMENT:

BLUBBERY HANDS

This experiment models blubber to test how effectively it protects the body from cold. Scientists often create test models, either in real life or using computer programs.

This is a messy experiment. Wash your hands after you have finished.

Suet is normally made of animal fat, but you can also buy vegetarian suet made from plant oils.

ASK

How does blubber keep animals warm in icy, cold habitats?

TEST

• Half-fill the bowl with cold water and ice cubes to make a model of an icy polar sea.
• Take two plastic food bags and almost fill one with suet.
• Put one hand in the suet bag, surrounded by suet, and one in the other bag.
• Ask someone to secure the bags around your wrists with elastic bands.
• Stick both hands in the icy water. How long can you keep them in?

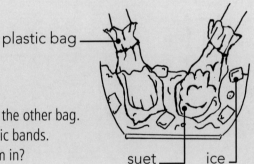

plastic bag

suet   ice

OBSERVE

How do your hands feel? Is there a difference?

MEASURE

Use the stopwatch to time how long you can keep each hand in the water.

WHAT NEXT?

Fat is an insulator, meaning it's not a good conductor, or carrier, of heat. So it stops heat escaping from inside the body. Try testing other substances, such as cotton wool, rice, butter or yoghurt.

Polar bears are excellent swimmers. Their layer of blubber keeps them from freezing in icy Arctic waters.

KEYSTONE SPECIES

Sometimes a species improves the habitat it lives in. When a living thing is key to the ecosystem working well, scientists call it a **keystone species**.

For example, honeybees are a keystone species. They pollinate flowers, spreading pollen from one to another. This allows plants to make seeds and fruit so they can reproduce. Bees helping plants to survive creates food and habitats for many other creatures too – aphids, ants, rabbits, butterflies, birds and so on.

Yellow pollen grains stick to the honeybee's body and brush off onto the next flower it visits.

The sea otter is a keystone species. It eats sea urchins – animals related to starfish.

Sea urchins eat **kelp** stems. If there are too many sea urchins, kelp forests can be destroyed.

Kelp forests are habitats for marine life. By eating sea urchins, sea otters help kelp forests and other animals.

A large, tall, clear container
Soil or potting compost
Rubber or gardening gloves
Sand
Dead leaves or
vegetable peelings
Earthworms

SCIENCE EXPERIMENT:

WORM HABITAT

Earthworms are a keystone species. They mix up the soil and make channels that let air and water in. This makes a better habitat for plants' roots to grow in and for animals to live in. To see how they do this, make a worm habitat.

You can collect earthworms outdoors, especially after heavy rain. However, it's also easy and quite cheap to order live earthworms online. They are sold for use in compost bins.

Wear gloves when handling soil or worms and wash your hands afterwards.

soil

Ask

What do worms do to the soil?

Test

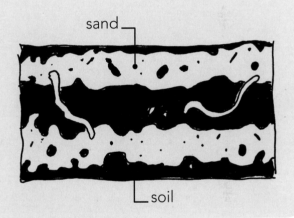

sand

soil

- To make your worm habitat, fill your container with thick layers of soil, then sand, then soil, and so on.
- Add a little water to keep the habitat damp (but don't flood it).
- Add your earthworms, then put some dead leaves or vegetable peelings on top.
- Keep your worm habitat somewhere quite dark and cool, like a garage or shed.

Observe

Check the habitat each day to see what the worms do and what happens to the soil.

Measure

How long does it take for the soil to get fully mixed together? After two weeks, tip your worms and soil out into a garden border or vegetable patch.

WHAT NEXT?

You could take a photo of the habitat each day to show how it changes. If you have a magnifying glass, you could also look at the soil closely to see if anything else is living there.

Worms have long, smooth bodies that are adapted for burrowing through soil.

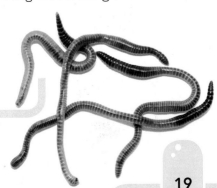

HOW TREES HELP

If we remove part of a habitat, it can have a serious effect on the ecosystem there. This is especially true for trees. Cutting them down can destroy habitats, known as **habitat loss**. All the living things there lose their home, and have to move elsewhere or die out.

A tree that took years to grow is cut down in minutes by a lumberjack with a chainsaw.

TREES CREATE HABITATS

Trees are living things that are also a habitat for many other organisms. Birds, squirrels, insects, snakes, frogs, fungi and monkeys can live in their branches, bark or leaves.

Trees also hold soil in place with their roots. The soil is a habitat for other, smaller plants, as well as bacteria, fungi and burrowing animals.

Tree roots reach a long way into the soil and burrowing animals, like this groundhog, often make their homes among them.

SCIENCE EXPERIMENT:

SAVING THE SOIL

This experiment uses a model to look at the way trees hold soil in place on hillsides. You'll need to do this experiment outdoors!

YOU WILL NEED:

2 cardboard boxes, such as shoeboxes
2 large trays
Soil or potting compost
Rubber or gardening gloves
20 plastic forks
Watering can and water

ASK

How do trees and their roots affect the soil on hillsides?

OBSERVE

What happens to the soil in each box?

MEASURE

Measure how much soil runs out of each box and collects in the tray.

TEST

- Make two model hillsides by filling the two boxes with soil.
- In one box, stick all the plastic forks into the soil to represent trees, with the prongs down to act as roots.
- Press the soil in both boxes down firmly. Then tear or cut a section out of the front of each box, like this.

soil ____   ____ fork

- Stand the open end of each box in a tray, and prop the other end up on a step or stone, so they are on a slope.
- Use the watering can to sprinkle the same amount of water over each box to represent rain.

WHAT NEXT?

Can you see how the fork 'trees' helped to keep the soil in place? What do you think is the best way to save hillside habitats from destruction?

A combination of few trees, heavy rain and the force of gravity caused this landslide in China.

BALANCING THE NUMBERS

In an ecosystem, one living thing eats another, which eats another, and so on, in a sequence called a **food chain**.

This is an example of a simple food chain.

plant grows

hare eats plant

cougar eats hare

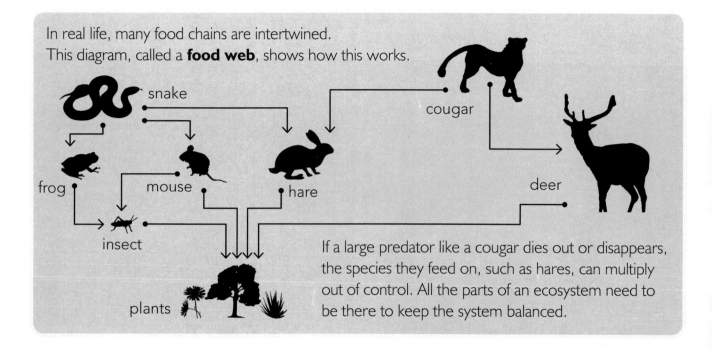

In real life, many food chains are intertwined. This diagram, called a **food web**, shows how this works.

snake

cougar

frog

mouse

hare

deer

insect

plants

If a large predator like a cougar dies out or disappears, the species they feed on, such as hares, can multiply out of control. All the parts of an ecosystem need to be there to keep the system balanced.

If you don't have counters, you can use coins or bits of paper.

YOU WILL NEED:

2 players
Lots of game counters in 2 different colours

SCIENCE EXPERIMENT:

POPULATION GAME

In this experimental game, two players represent cougars and hares feeding and breeding.

 ASK

How do predators like cougars help ecosystems stay in balance?

 OBSERVE

Keep playing and see what happens. Does the ecosystem self-regulate and stay balanced?

 TEST

- One player is Cougar, and one is Hare.
- Start by setting out two cougar counters and 25 hare counters.
- On each go, Cougar adds or removes counters so there is always one cougar per ten hares, to represent cougars breeding when they have enough food.
  Examples:
  25 hares = 2 cougars
  32 hares = 3 cougars, and so on.
- Then, Cougar should 'eat' (remove) six hares for each cougar. So if there are two cougars, remove 12 hares.
- Now it's Hare's turn. On each go, Hare must double the number of counters it has to represent the hares breeding.
  Example:
  13 hares double to make 26 hares.
- Now it's Cougar's turn again.

 MEASURE

Write down the numbers of cougars and hares after each turn. Can you spot any patterns? Finally, remove Cougar from the game. Hare simply doubles the counters on each go. How many goes does it take for the hares to increase to 100?

WHAT NEXT?

With no cougars, can you work out how many turns it would take to reach a million hares? Could you design a game with three or more species/players?

A cougar chases a snowshoe hare across a snowy landscape.

BUILDING THE ENVIRONMENT

Some living things actually construct habitats themselves. They change the place they live in, building structures that create a new environment for other living things.

Coral reef dwellers include seaweed, octopuses, fish, turtles and crabs.

For example, coral polyps are tiny sea creatures, related to jellyfish and sea anemones. They live in groups, or colonies, and grow a shared, hard shell, known as coral. As old coral polyps die, new ones build more coral on top. Over time, this makes large structures in the sea called coral reefs. They become a habitat for a whole ecosystem.

These white coral polyps live inside this orange coral shell.

BUILDING A DAM

Beavers are also amazing animal builders. These mammals build dams across streams and rivers, using logs, branches and mud to make areas of deeper water where they can avoid predators.

Beavers also build a home, called a lodge, in their river.

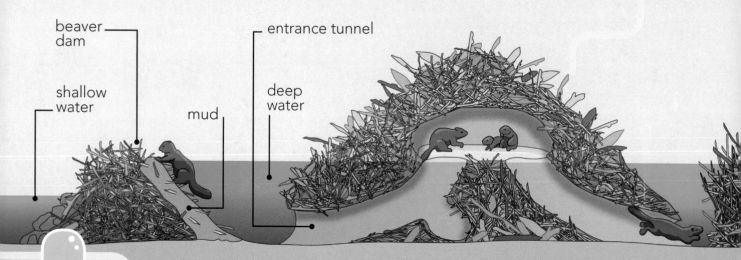

beaver dam

entrance tunnel

shallow water

deep water

mud

BEAVER DAM

In this experiment, you can build a model beaver dam to see how it changes the flow of water in a stream.

YOU WILL NEED:

Modelling clay
Large tray or plank
Water and a jug
Matchsticks or tiny twigs
Sand

A beaver arranges branches and twigs to construct a dam.

 Ask

How do beavers change their environment by building dams?

 Test

- First, use modelling clay to form a long, V-shaped valley along the tray or plank.
- Outdoors, prop the tray or plank up at one end so it is gently sloping.
- Test the valley by pouring water from the jug into the higher end to make a stream.
- Use sand, and twigs or matchsticks to block the valley with a beaver-style dam.
- Pour water in again to see what happens.

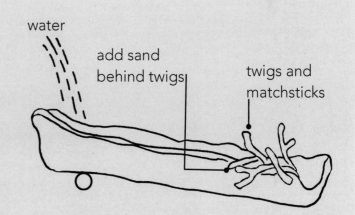

water

add sand behind twigs

twigs and matchsticks

 Observe

Look at how the dam works to hold back the water and let it through more slowly.

Measure

Compare the depth of the water behind the dam to the water downstream from it.

WHAT NEXT?

When you're playing in a real stream, you could try making a real dam with stones and sticks (as long as it's safe and there are adults with you, of course!).

Think about how a beaver dam creates an area of slow-flowing water. How could this help other living things?

CLIMATE CHANGE

Habitats and biomes depend on their **climate**, or the weather patterns where they are, staying roughly the same. Living things are adapted to the temperature, rainfall and sunshine levels of their habitat.

Weather and seasons vary, of course, and that is normal. But if the climate changes overall, habitats change too, and some living things will struggle to survive. For example, if the climate became warmer and drier, a pond could dry up. It would no longer be a good home for fish, frogs, ducks and water weeds.

Sunflowers need a sunny climate to help them grow.

GLOBAL WARMING

Over time, Earth's climate changes naturally. In the past it has been much warmer or colder than it is now – during ice ages, for example. These changes happen very slowly, and many species adapt to them.

However, Earth is now getting warmer at a faster rate – often known as **global warming**. Scientists think this is because of gases released into the **atmosphere** by our factories, power stations and vehicles. Some of them, called **greenhouse gases**, trap the Sun's heat and make the world warmer. This is called the **greenhouse effect**.

A pond habitat supports many plant and animal species. If a pond dries up, living things can lose their home.

A power station releases polluting gases into the atmosphere.

SCIENCE EXPERIMENT:

GREENHOUSE MODEL

A real greenhouse is warm on the inside because the glass allows heat in, but prevents some of the heat from escaping. This experiment models the greenhouse effect to show how it works.

greenhouse _____

 ASK

How does the greenhouse effect make the climate warmer?

 TEST

- Find a bright or sunny area on a table or on the floor.
- Put one thermometer under the bowl, and the other next to the bowl.
- Make sure they are both in the same amount of sunlight or daylight.

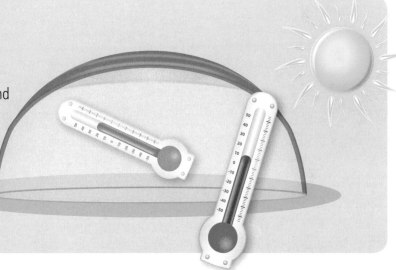

 OBSERVE

After half an hour, check the temperatures on the thermometers.

 MEASURE

What was the difference inside the bowl, compared to outside it?

WHAT NEXT?

Greenhouse gases in the Earth's atmosphere act like the bowl (and like a greenhouse). They let heat in, but stop some of it from escaping, so the temperature rises. Can you think of good ways to reduce the greenhouse effect?

READING YOUR RESULTS

When scientists do experiments, they get results. Even if nothing happened as they expected, that is a result too! All results can be useful, but it is important to understand them. Here are some guidelines that scientists use to learn from their results.

USE A CONTROL

A **control** is a normal version of the set-up, without the thing that is being tested. In the case of the Blubbery Hands experiment (p.17), the thing being tested is the 'blubber'. The 'control' is the hand not covered in 'blubber'.

It's really important that apart from the thing being tested, the control version matches the test version in every way. So you put the control hand into the same bowl of water, in the same type of bag, at the same time. Then you know that any differences in your results are purely down to the blubber.

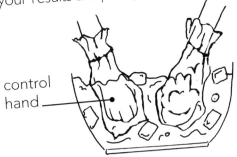

control hand

REPEAT AND VERIFY

An experiment may work well once, but what if that was a fluke? So that they can be sure of their results, scientists often repeat and **verify** an experiment several times.

CHECK FOR BIAS

If you're *really* hoping for an exciting result, it's possible you might accidentally-on-purpose 'help' your experiment along by ignoring something that doesn't fit with what you wanted. This is called **bias** and can happen without you even realising it. A good scientist always tries to avoid bias.

OUTLIERS

What if you were conducting the Habitat Trail experiment (p. 9) in your garden, and you spotted a lion?

Besides running away, you'd probably be quite surprised, as lions do not normally live in gardens. This unusual result is called an **outlier**. Scientists have to check outliers carefully and work out why they have happened. For example, the lion might have escaped from a zoo.

KEEPING RECORDS

Writing down the details of each experiment and what the results were is essential for scientists. Not only does it help explain their work to others; it also means they can use results to look for patterns. For example, do soft foods in your mould garden (p. 13) grow mould faster or slower than hard foods?

MAKING MISTAKES

If you spot a mistake, start the experiment again. It would be an even bigger mistake to use the results from a badly run experiment.

However, if a mistake makes something interesting happen, you could set up a new experiment to test for that instead. Many important discoveries have been made this way. For example, **antibiotics** were discovered when mould grew in an old testing dish that hadn't been washed, and a scientist noticed that it killed the bacteria there.

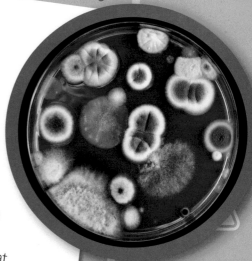

GLOSSARY

adapt To change to become well-suited to a habitat.

antibiotics Medicines that kill bacteria in the body.

atmosphere The layer of gases surrounding the Earth.

bacteria Simple life forms that are made of a single cell and can multiply rapidly. Some bacteria carry infectious diseases, while others are harmless.

bias The tendency to look for what you want or expect to see from an experiment.

biome A large area of a main type of habitat, such as desert, ocean or forest.

blubber A thick layer of fat under the skin that protects against cold temperatures.

camouflage Markings, shapes or colours that blend in with the surroundings.

climate The usual weather conditions in a particular place.

climate change Long-term changes in weather patterns on Earth, or in a particular place.

control A standard version of something, used in an experiment to compare with the thing being tested.

deciduous Refers to trees and shrubs that lose their leaves in autumn and winter and grow new leaves in spring.

ecosystem A habitat and all the living things in it, which work together as a system.

endangered At risk of dying out and becoming extinct.

environment The surroundings in which an organism lives.

evolution A process of gradual change over a series of steps or generations.

extinct No longer existing.

food chain A sequence of living things in which one eats the next, which eats the next, and so on.

food web A network of the living things in an ecosystem, showing who feeds on what.

fruiting body The part of a fungus that grows outwards from the mycelium and produces spores. A mushroom is a fruiting body.

fungi A group of living things that includes mushrooms, moulds and yeast.

generation A group of living things that live at the same time. Their children are the next generation, their grandchildren are the generation after that, and so on.

global warming The current, unusually fast rise in Earth's temperature, caused by an increase in greenhouse gases from pollution.

greenhouse effect The way gases in Earth's atmosphere trap heat.

greenhouse gases Gases, such as carbon dioxide, that trap heat in Earth's atmosphere.

habitat loss The destruction or disappearance of a habitat.

kelp A type of large seaweed.

keystone species A species that helps its ecosystem and the living things in it.

mycelium A network of thread-like roots that a fungus uses to feed.

organism A scientific name for a living thing.

outlier A very unusual or unexpected result that is unlike the other results for an experiment.

Petri dish A shallow, circular, see-through dish used by scientists for growing bacteria.

predator A living thing that hunts and eats other living things.

prey A living thing that is eaten by another living thing.

savanna Grassy plains with few trees in tropical areas.

species The scientific name for a particular type of living thing.

tundra A cold habitat where no trees grow, only low-growing shrubs, mosses and grasses.

venomous An animal, such as a snake or a wasp, that can inject venom into a prey animal through a bite or a sting.

verify To check and prove an experiment works.

BOOKS

A Little Bit of Dirt: 55+ Science and Art Activities to Reconnect Children with Nature
by Asia Citro (The Innovation Press)

Eyewitness: Climate Change
(Dorling Kindersley)

Moving up with Science: Habitats
by Peter Riley (Franklin Watts)

Symbiosis: How Different Animals Relate
by Bobbie Kalman (Crabtree)

Planet Earth: Ecosystems
by Andy Horsley (Ticktock)

Other books in this series:

Science Skills Sorted: Plants
Science Skills Sorted: Human and Animal Bodies
Science Skills Sorted: Life Cycles
Science Skills Sorted: Evolution and Classification
Science Skills Sorted: Rocks and Fossils

WEBSITES

Brainpop: Scientific method
https://www.brainpop.com/science/scientificinquiry/scientificmethod/

School of Dragons: Scientific method worksheets
http://www.schoolofdragons.com/how-to-train-your-dragon/the-scientific-method/scientific-method-worksheets

PlanetPals: Habitats
http://www.planetpals.com/habitats.html

Enchanted Learning: Biomes
http://www.enchantedlearning.com/biomes/

Kids Do Ecology
http://kids.nceas.ucsb.edu/index.html

Blue Planet Biomes
http://www.blueplanetbiomes.org/

What's It Like Where You Live?
http://www.mbgnet.net/

Every effort has been made by the Publishers to ensure that the websites in this book are suitable for children, that they are of the highest educational value, and that they contain no inappropriate or offensive material. However, because of the nature of the Internet, it is impossible to guarantee that the contents of these sites will not be altered. We strongly advise that Internet access is supervised by a responsible adult.

INDEX

adaptations 4, 10–11, 16
animals, endangered 6
antibiotics 29

bacteria 8, 20, 29
beavers 24–25
bias, avoiding 28
biomes 5, 26
blubber 16–17, 28

camouflage 10, 14–15
caterpillars 10
climate 6, 26–27
climate change 6, 26–27
controls, using 28
coral reefs 15, 24
corals/coral polyps 6, 24
cougars 22–23

deserts 4, 5, 14, 15, 16

earthworms 19
edelweiss 16
evolution 10, 16
experiments, conducting
  7, 28–29

fennec foxes 16
flounders 14
food chains 22–23
food webs 22
forests 4, 5, 6, 15
fungi 9, 12–13, 20

giant squid 11
greenhouse effect 26–27
greenhouse gases 26–27
groundhogs 20

habitat loss 4, 20–21
habitats, types of 4–5
hares 22–23
honeybees 18

kelp 18
keystone species 18–19

moulds 8, 9, 12–13, 29
mycelium 12

oceans 4, 6, 11, 16, 17, 24
outliers 29

pebble plants 14
polar bears 16, 17
pollination 18
predators 14, 26–27
prey 14

rock pools 11
roots 12, 19, 20, 21

sand cats 4, 5
science investigations/
  experiments:
    beaver dam 25
    blubbery hands 17, 28

creating camouflage 15
greenhouse model 27
habitat trail 9, 29
mould garden 13, 29
pond dipping 11
population game 23
saving the soil 21
worm habitat 19
sea otters 18
sea urchins 18
shrews, common 13
silverfish 8
spores 12

trees 9, 20–21

warming, global 26
water boatman 11
whales 4, 16

SCIENCE SKILLS SORTED
These are the lists of contents for the titles in the Science Skills Sorted series:

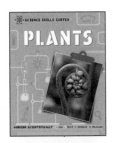

PLANTS

What makes a plant a plant? • The science of plants • Working scientifically • Seeds • Plant defence • What plants need to grow • Surviving a drought • Water content • How leaves work • Helping nature • Flowers and seeds • Autumn colours • Cloning plants • Reading your results • Glossary and further information • Index

HABITATS

What is a habitat? • The science of habitats • Working scientifically • Wildlife habitats • Adaptations • Moving in • Blending in • Extreme habitats • Keystone species • How trees help • Balancing the numbers • Building the environment • Climate change • Reading your results • Glossary and further information • Index

LIFE CYCLES

What is a life cycle? • The science of life cycles • Working scientifically • From seed to seed • Eggs and babies • Metamorphosis • Finding a mate • Dividing bacteria • Budding yeast • Spreading out • Generations • Life cycle maths • Hitching a ride • Reading your results • Glossary and further information • Index

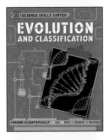

EVOLUTION AND CLASSIFICATION

What is evolution? • The science of evolution • Working scientifically • Evolution in action • Survival of the fittest • Finding food • Adapting to habitats • Winning a mate • Genes and generations • Classification • Sorting it out • Living relatives • The DNA key • Reading your results • Glossary and further information • Index

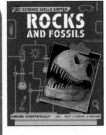

ROCKS AND FOSSILS

What are rocks, minerals and fossils? • The science of rocks and fossils • Working scientifically • Types of rock • Rocks and water • Minerals and crystals • How hard? • Weathering and erosion • Expanding ice • Making mountains • Volcanoes and earthquakes • How fossils form • Fossil puzzles • Reading your results • Glossary and further information • Index

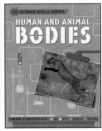

HUMAN AND ANIMAL BODIES

Humans and other animals? • Studying humans and animals • Working scientifically • Bones • Moving on land • Built to fly • Super streamlined • Sharp sight • Locating sound • Interesting smell • Teeth and beaks • Breathing • Unique individuals • Reading your results • Glossary and further information • Index

First Published in 1979 by
Sampson Low, Berkshire House,
Queen Street, Maidenhead,
Berkshire SL6 1NF

SBN 562 00117 4

Designed by Peter Kenny Ltd., Ewell
Filmset by Tradespools Ltd., and Filmtype Services Ltd.
Printed by Waterlows (Dunstable) Ltd.

AUDREY ELLIS

Lunch
and
Supper
MENUS

MENU PLANNERS

Sampson Low

Contents

Cook's guide — ten
Introduction — eleven
Useful cookery terms — twelve
Introduction to menus — fifteen

1
Chicken liver terrine with French bread
Tossed lettuce salad
Apricot ice cream — sixteen

2
Prawn and olive starter
Creamy vegetable casserole
Orange sorbet shells — eighteen

3
Sorrel-stuffed eggs
Tourte au chou
Apple snow — twenty

4
Orange-basted chicken with baby beetroots
Quick scalloped cauliflower
Caramel snow eggs — twenty-two

5
Turkey and apricot pilau
Salade aux chapons
Cider and sultana sponge pudding — twenty-four

6
Southern fried chicken with concasse of tomatoes
Ribbon noodles
Courgettes and mushrooms
Rhubarb and mandarin tart — twenty-six

7
Sole with spiced butter
Asparagus with Orange hollandaise sauce
Gooseberry fool with ice cream — twenty-eight

8
Chicken and chips in a basket
Radish salad
Plum flan with raisin sauce — thirty

9
Oysters with croquettes
Crisp celery salad
Zabaglione — thirty-two

10
Aubergines in cream cheese
Herring potato balls with dill
Loganberry ice cream — thirty-four

11	Artichoke omelette Rhubarb and orange fool	*thirty-six*
12	Cheesey Charlies with spiced cherry sauce Lettuce and cucumber salad	*thirty-seven*
13	Beef stew with apricot dumplings French beans Grape and coconut flan	*thirty-eight*
14	Roast lamb with lemon chutney sauce Minted new potatoes and peas Greengage strudel	*forty*
15	Scallop mélange au gratin Fluffy boiled rice with dill weed Blackberry and pear pudding	*forty-two*
16	Spanish tortilla omelette Peach toasts	*forty-four*
17	Fish in capered mayonnaise Pan chicken and vegetables Mixed salad Coffee and nut ice cream	*forty-six*
18	Beef and egg pies Green salad Vicarage trifle	*forty-eight*
19	Mackerel with apple stuffing Courgettes with black olives Pancake soufflé	*fifty*
20	Pasta with pork stroganoff Bel Paese cheese with French bread	*fifty-two*
21	Spiced ham croquettes Sliced fresh peaches with cream	*fifty-three*
22	Curried fish kedgeree Blackberry and apple coupes	*fifty-four*
23	Courgette salad Chicken and ham patties	*fifty-five*

24   Fried cod with beetroot and horseradish cream
Fried potatoes
Pear and apricot whip   *fifty-six*

25   Sausages Somerset style
Cheddar cheese platter with celery hearts   *fifty-eight*

26   Stuffed courgettes with rice
Fresh pears with cream   *fifty-nine*

27   Fish duglère
Creamed potatoes
Blueberry pancake layer   *sixty*

28   Hot German potato salad
Green bean and frankfurter salad
Jambon aux fonds d'artichauts   *sixty-two*

29   Chicken livers in Madeira sauce
Tossed watercress salad
Chocolate orange dessert   *sixty-four*

30   Raised game pie with Cran-apple relish
Red coleslaw with celery
Stilton cheese platter   *sixty-six*

31   Hansel's curry soup
Glazed gammon with carrots
Buttered pasta shells
Sliced bananas with cream   *sixty-eight*

32   Lamb with lemon herb stuffing
Maçedoine of vegetables and new potatoes
Pineapple ginger pudding with
Pineapple sauce   *seventy*

33   Golden potato-topped pie with onions
Green peas
Beignets   *seventy-two*

34   Chicken with capers
Cauliflower florets
Chestnut soufflé
Coffee liqueur sauce   *seventy-four*

35 **Sausage and butterbean quickies**
Orange 'n lemon beetroot *seventy-six*
Frozen date and nut pie

36 **Nutty pork crescents**
Tomato glazed chicory *seventy-eight*
Chilled pineapple poll

37 **Veal birds**
Golden grapefruit sponge with *eighty*
Grapefruit sauce

38 **Fish pie with swede purée**
Baked apples with maple syrup *eighty-two*

39 **Braised beef with mustard**
Baked potatoes *eighty-three*
Mincemeat cobbler

40 **Brunch kidneys**
Scrambled eggs with crumbled crispy bacon *eighty-four*
Poppy seed plait
Hungarian bubble loaf
Almond apricot conserve

41 **Basting sauce**
Lamburgers *eighty-six*
Kebabs
Potato and bacon salad
Red and white coleslaw

42 **Melon with Parma ham**
Italian supper dish *eighty-eight*
Sorrento salad
Gorgonzola cheese with peaches

Adding inspiration to cheese *ninety*
Acknowledgments *ninety-two*
Index *ninety-three*

Cook's guide

In this book, quantities are given in Metric, Imperial and American measures. Where ingredients are differently described in the U.S.A., the alternative name is given in brackets. All menus are to serve 4 unless otherwise indicated.

Spoon measures: In general, teaspoons and table-spoons make handy measures, although not always completely accurate. 3 teaspoons equal 1 tablespoon and 8 tablespoons equal about 150 ml/¼ Imperial pint. (If you use a standard measuring spoon, it actually holds 17.7 ml.) The American tablespoon is slightly smaller (holding 14.2 ml) therefore occasionally an extra tablespoon is indicated in the American column of measures. All spoon measures are taken as being level.

Liquid measures: Quantities are given in millilitres, pints and American cup measures. The American pint contains only 16 fl oz compared with the Imperial pint which contains 20 fl oz, and the American measuring cup contains 8 fl oz.

Can sizes: Since there is no absolute conformity among manufacturers in their can sizes, the exact quantity required is indicated. If, for example, a 396 g/14 oz can of tomatoes is required, the nearest equivalent you can find on the shelves may be up to 50g/2 oz larger or smaller. Generally speaking, this does not affect the success of the recipe.

Oven temperature chart   Few ovens are accurately adjusted. If you are not satisfied with the results given by your oven, test the temperature range with an oven thermometer and set your dial accordingly.

Oven temperature chart

	°F	°C	Gas Mark
Very cool	225	110	¼
	250	130	½
Cool	275	140	1
	300	150	2
Moderate	325	170	3
	350	180	4
Moderately hot	375	190	5
	400	200	6
Hot	425	220	7
	450	230	8
Very hot	475	240	9

Introduction

To some people, lunches and suppers are main meals with a casual approach. To others, lunch implies a roast joint followed by a pudding, while supper suggests macaroni cheese or Welsh rarebit. The menus you will find in this book are rather more imaginative and take a far wider view of the many delicious meals you might enjoy which are not formal dinners. Some of my favourite meals are very light indeed – perhaps an unusual artichoke omelette followed by a delicate fruit fool. Others are more substantial but just a little different from the 'run of the mill'. For instance, the classic roast lamb with minted new potatoes and peas gets a lift with an accompanying lemon chutney sauce and there is a fruit strudel to follow instead of the anticipated deep dish pie. Not only will you extend your repertoire as a cook when you try out some of these new dishes, you will discover how easy it is to mix and match different dishes to make up a well-balanced meal.

Cooking ought to be a pleasure, not merely a chore. You can attempt any of the recipes in this book without strewing your kitchen with saucepans of all sizes, or leaving your sink piled high with numerous utensils. But the range of these menus extends from simple quickly-prepared family meals to far more elegant occasions when you take pride in entertaining.

Audrey Ellis

Useful cookery terms

Adventures in cooking occasionally fail, not because you have taken insufficient care in following the recipe, but because you have misinterpreted some part of the instructions. A knowledge of the exact meaning of simple terms in everyday use and also the less usual ones is a form of insurance against your efforts in the kitchen being disappointing. Then the mysteries of the restaurant menu disappear when, for example, you know in advance that a fricassée is sure to be a white meat stew rather than a brown one. This carefully chosen list of terms includes those which require the most knowledgeable interpretation when you are cooking, or when you eat out.

Arrowroot: A thickening agent which gives a clearer and more transparent finish than cornflour (cornstarch).

Aspic: A clear savoury jelly prepared from powder, crystals or simply from setting strong bone stock.

Bain-marie: A water bath which is used to stand casseroles or other cooking vessels in, either to keep food hot or to protect it while cooking. A roasting tin can be used as a bain-marie.

Bake blind: Bake pastry by filling uncooked shell with foil and dried beans and baking in the oven.

Barbecue: The Spanish name for a style of cooking, originally roasting a whole animal but now used to describe outdoor cooking of any food over a charcoal fire.

Bard: To wrap a solid piece of meat which is rather lean, with thin sheets of animal fat, held in place either with skewers or string.

Baste: To spoon fat, or sauce, over food during cooking to keep it moist.

Beurre manié: Butter and flour kneaded together in the proportion of 3:1 then used for thickening sauces and soups. Sauce should be cooked and stirred only long enough to thicken and cook the flour.

Candy: To preserve a fruit by impregnating it with boiling sugar syrup.

Caramel: A preparation made by boiling sugar syrup until it is rich straw to light amber in colour when it can be used for flavouring, or lining moulds for baked egg custards.

Chantilly: A name applicable to whipped cream incorporating sugar and vanilla flavouring.

Coat: To cover food for frying with flour, egg and breadcrumbs, or with batter.

Compôte: Any fresh fruit cooked in a sugar syrup.

Concasse: Finely chopped tomato flesh from which peel and seeds have been removed.

Consommé: Chicken or meat stock which has been reduced to concentrate it and clarified. It should be strong enough to set firmly when cold.

Court bouillon: A fish stock flavoured with wine or vinegar and sliced onion, herbs, etc. to taste.

Cream: To beat fat and sugar with a wooden spoon or mixer until light and fluffy.

Crêpe: A delicate pancake.

Croûtons: Small cubes of stale bread fried golden brown in a mixture of butter and oil, or toasted.

Custard: May be made with milk, eggs and sugar, or with milk, sugar and vanilla-flavoured cornflour.

Derind: To remove thick skin from bacon or pork.

Deseed: To remove core, membranes and seeds from peppers or tomatoes.

Dot: To place small pieces of butter evenly over the surface of food such as sliced potatoes before cooking to prevent drying and give a good colour.

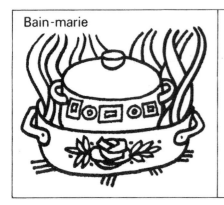  

Bain-marie | Bard | Chantilly

Double boiler or saucepan: A pan containing food fitted into a lower pan containing water thus preventing food from coming into direct contact with the heat source. A substitute can be contrived using a pudding basin and ordinary saucepan.

Drain: To remove excess liquid from food.

Dredge: To sprinkle food with a dry ingredient through a sifter.

Emulsion: A suspension made by combining a thickening agent with other ingredients, e.g. egg yolks and oil to make mayonnaise.

En croûte: Meat or fish partly cooked then baked in puff pastry.

Fines herbes: This denotes that a mixture of chopped fresh herbs has been added to a dish.

Flake: To break cooked fish into pieces with a fork without mashing.

Flamber: To pour ignited brandy or other spirit over food.

Fleurons: Crescent-shaped pieces of baked puff pastry used as a garnish.

Flute: To decorate pastry edges with finger and thumb or with a knife before baking.

Fondue: A hot cheese dish made with white wine used as a dip for small pieces of bread spiked on long forks. (Fondue bourguignonne – cubes of tender beef speared on long forks and immersed in a pan of very hot oil to cook.)

Garnish: Small items used to decorate a savoury dish, such as parsley and lemon slices.

Glaze: A sweet glaze of sugar syrup or sieved jam used to give a shiny surface to food; or a savoury glaze of reduced meat stock.

Grill: To cook food under direct heat in a grill (broiler).

Infuse: To steep flavouring ingredients in hot liquid.

Lard: To thread strips of pork fat through lean meat before cooking.

Liquidise: To process food in a blender until it becomes a smooth mixture or liquid.

Marinate: To soak food such as meat in a mixture of oil, acid (wine or vinegar) and seasonings to tenderise it and impart more flavour. The mixture is known as a marinade.

Parboil: To cook food such as vegetables in liquid until just softened. Final cooking to be completed by a different method.

Pipe: To press smooth food such as whipped cream through a pastry tube to produce a decorative result before serving.

Poach: To cook food such as white fish very gently in liquid to avoid it breaking up.

Purée: To pass food through a sieve or liquidise to a smooth consistency.

Reduce: To boil liquid hard to evaporate water and produce a stronger flavour.

Refresh: An old-fashioned term for pouring cold water over partly-cooked vegetables to preserve the brightness of colour.

Render: To melt down fat to obtain a smooth dripping, discarding small pieces of skin tissue.

Roux: A mixture of butter and flour combined over heat as a thickening for sauces.

Rub in: To cut fat into dry ingredients until the mixture resembles breadcrumbs.

Sauté: To fry food briskly in fat in a wide shallow pan until crisp and golden brown.

Sieve: To push food such as gooseberries through a strainer to remove skins and seeds.

Sift: To pass dry ingredients such as flour and ground spices through a sieve to remove lumps, mix them uniformly and introduce air to the food.

Simmer: To cook food in liquid at just below boiling point. Bubbles should rise occasionally and break just below the surface.

Skim: To remove scum or excess fat from the surface of liquid, such as a soup.

Spit roast: To roast a whole bird or joint on a large skewer which is turned mechanically under the heat source.

Steep: To let food stand in hot liquid to extract the flavour. (See infuse.)

Strain: To remove all particles of food from a liquid by pouring through a strainer.

Tenderise: To bat or beat slices of meat prior to cooking in order to break down the fibres and make the flesh more tender.

Toss: To lift and mix food lightly with two forks until coated with dressing or melted butter.

Trim: To cut away excess fat and skin from meat joints and chops, or remove the roots, leaves, etc. from vegetables.

Truss: To tie legs and wing tips of poultry into shape close to the body before cooking.

Vinaigrette or French (Italian) dressing: A classic combination of oil and vinegar in proportions of 2 parts oil to 1 part vinegar, seasoned to taste with salt, pepper and occasionally mustard. Used for salads.

Weight: To press pâtés or terrines with a weight while chilling to produce a firm close texture suitable for cutting.

Whisk: To combine and incorporate air into ingredients by beating, sometimes over heat while the mixture cooks.

14

These meal plans are extremely flexible, according to how much time you can devote to cooking.

Save preparation time by omitting the sweet course and offering fresh fruit instead. Or make them a little more substantial by introducing an additional vegetable or extra salad. Some suggestions for rounding out the menus such as 'tossed green salad' are given without recipes.

A fair proportion of the total recipe collection is for meals which will put no strain on the housekeeping budget. A few are frankly a little more extravagant and would be delightful for informal entertaining.

MENU 1

Chicken liver terrine with French bread
Tossed lettuce salad
Apricot ice cream

Chicken liver terrine

INGREDIENTS	METRIC	IMP.	U.S.
Chicken livers	575 g	1¼ lb	1¼ lb
Salt belly of pork	225 g	8 oz	½ lb
2 medium onions			
Stale bread	200 g	7 oz	3½ cups
2 eggs			
Salt and pepper			
3 sprigs of thyme			
4 tbspns brandy			
JELLY STOCK			
2 calves feet			
Water	1 litre+	2 pints	5 cups
White wine	300 ml	½ pint	1¼ cups
Sprig of thyme			
1 bay leaf			
1 small carrot, sliced			
1 small onion, sliced			
1 clove garlic			
2 tbspns brandy			
1 tbspn meat extract			

First make the jelly stock. Simmer the calves feet with all other ingredients and seasoning to taste in a saucepan, covered, for 2 hours. Reduce by rapid boiling to give 18 fl oz/½ litre/2¼ cups strained stock. Chop the chicken livers, mince the pork and onions. Break up the bread and soak it in a little of the stock. Mix together the minced pork mixture with the livers, bread, lightly beaten eggs, salt and pepper to taste. Strip the sprigs of thyme and add to the mixture with the brandy. Mix well. Turn into a small ovenproof terrine dish and smooth the top. Pour over a little of the stock and cook in a moderate oven (350°F, 180°C, Gas Mark 4) for about 45 minutes. Add just sufficient stock during cooking to prevent the mixture from becoming dry. Cool, pour over the remaining stock and chill until set.

Apricot ice cream

INGREDIENTS	METRIC	IMP.	U.S.
Ripe apricots	500 g	1¼ lb	1¼ lb
Sugar	100 g	4 oz	½ cup
Water	150 ml	¼ pint	½ cup
1 tbspn ginger syrup			
1 tbspn chopped stem ginger			
Double [whipping] cream	450 ml	¾ pint	2 cups

Halve the apricots, remove stones, and steam until tender. Sieve or liquidise in a blender. Meanwhile, slowly heat the sugar in the water until dissolved, then simmer gently to reduce by about half. Add the ginger syrup and cool. Stir in the apricot purée and the chopped ginger. Whip the cream and fold it in lightly. Pour the mixture into a freezing tray, cover with foil or cling wrap (to prevent loss of the delicate flavour) and freeze until crystals begin to form. Remove from the freezing tray and beat well, return to the tray and freeze until solid. Serve small portions of this rich ice cream with vanilla flavoured wafer biscuits.

Prawn and olive starter
Creamy vegetable casserole
Orange sorbet shells

Prawn and olive starter

INGREDIENTS	METRIC	IMP.	U.S.
1 lettuce heart			
Canned anchovy fillets	50 g	2 oz	2 oz
6 stuffed green olives			
3 tomatoes			
Peeled prawns [shrimp]	75 g	3 oz	$\frac{3}{4}$ cup
DRESSING			
Oil	6 tbspns	6 tbspns	$\frac{1}{2}$ cup
2 tbspns lemon juice			
Salt and pepper			
Pinch of dry mustard			
Pinch of sugar			
1 hard-boiled egg to garnish			

Tear the lettuce into small pieces. Divide between 3 individual bowls. Drain the anchovies. Halve the olives. Peel and quarter the tomatoes and remove the seeds. Add to the lettuce with the anchovies, prawns and olives. Whisk together all the ingredients for the dressing and pour over the salads. Slice the hard-boiled egg and use to garnish the starters. Serves 3.

Creamy vegetable casserole

INGREDIENTS	METRIC	IMP.	U.S.
French [green] beans	225 g	8 oz	$\frac{1}{2}$ lb
Button onions	225 g	8 oz	$\frac{1}{2}$ lb
Corn kernels	350 g	12 oz	$\frac{3}{4}$ lb
Butter	50 g	2 oz	$\frac{1}{4}$ cup
Flour	3 tbspns	3 tbspns	$\frac{1}{4}$ cup—
Milk	6 tbspns	6 tbspns	$\frac{1}{2}$ cup
Single cream [half & half]	6 tbspns	6 tbspns	$\frac{1}{2}$ cup
Dry white wine	150 ml	$\frac{1}{4}$ pint	$\frac{1}{2}$ cup
$\frac{1}{2}$ tspn dill weed			
$\frac{1}{2}$ tspn salt			
Pinch pepper			
$\frac{1}{2}$ tspn prepared mustard			
$\frac{1}{2}$ tspn Worcestershire sauce			
Grated cheese	100 g	4 oz	1 cup

Cut the beans into 2 inch/5 cm lengths and cook with the onions and corn in a little boiling salted water until tender. In a clean pan, melt the butter, stir in the flour. Gradually add milk, cream, wine, herbs and seasonings and bring to the boil, stirring constantly. Add the drained vegetables and turn into an ovenproof dish. Sprinkle with the cheese and bake in a moderate oven (350°F, 180°C, Gas Mark 4) for about 20 minutes. Serves 3.

Orange sorbet shells

INGREDIENTS	METRIC	IMP.	U.S.
4 large oranges			
1 lemon			
Water	600 ml	1 pint	$2\frac{1}{2}$ cups
Sugar	225 g	8 oz	1 cup
Little egg white			
Sprigs of mint			

Cut the tops from 3 of the oranges and scoop out the flesh, taking care not to damage the 'shells'. Finely grate the rind from the remaining orange and from the lemon and squeeze the juice from both. Place the orange flesh, rinds and juices in a saucepan with the water and sugar and stir over gentle heat until the sugar has dissolved, then boil hard for 5 minutes. Strain into a shallow container and cool. Freeze until slushy. Turn out and beat well. Whisk the egg white until firm, add 2 heaped tablespoons to the frozen fruit mixture and fold in. Spoon into the orange 'shells', stand in a polythene container and cover with lid. Pack any remaining mixture separately. Freeze until firm. When required for serving, place the orange 'shells' on a plate and spoon a little extra frozen sorbet on top of each. Defrost for about 20 minutes and serve decorated with sprigs of mint. Serves 3.

MENU 3

Sorrel-stuffed eggs
Tourte au chou
Apple snow

Sorrel-stuffed eggs

INGREDIENTS	METRIC	IMP.	U.S.
4 eggs			
Sorrel leaves	50 g	2 oz	2 oz
Butter	25 g	1 oz	2 tbspns
3 tbspns cream cheese			
1 tspn grated [minced] onion			
Salt and pepper			
8 peeled shrimps			
Watercress leaves			

Hard boil the eggs, shell and cut in half. Scoop out the yolk. Cook the sorrel in the butter in a tightly covered pan for about 8 minutes, or until tender. Drain and chop very finely. Mash the cooked egg yolks with the sorrel and cream cheese. Beat in the minced onion and seasonings. Spoon the mixture into the egg white halves. Top each egg half with a shrimp for garnish. Arrange on a bed of watercress leaves. Serve with thinly sliced brown bread and butter.

Tourte au chou

INGREDIENTS	METRIC	IMP.	U.S.
Shortcrust pastry [basic pie dough]	275 g	10 oz	10 oz
1 small green cabbage			
Cooked meat	350 g	12 oz	12 oz
Streaky [side] bacon slices	50 g	2 oz	2 oz
1 large onion			
Sprig parsley			
Butter	50 g	2 oz	$\frac{1}{4}$ cup
$\frac{1}{2}$ tspn dried thyme			
Pinch ground allspice			
Salt and pepper			
1 egg			

Roll out two-thirds of the pastry to line a deep 8 inch/20 cm flan tin. Chop the cabbage finely and blanch in fast boiling salted water for 8 minutes. Drain well. Meanwhile, mince together the meat, bacon, onion and parsley. Melt the butter, turn the meat mixture in this, adding the herbs, spices and seasoning to taste, until well blended and lightly browned. Place half the cabbage in the flan case, cover with the meat mixture and put the remaining cabbage on top. Roll out rest of pastry to make a lid, slightly larger than the flan case. Use lid to cover the tourte, dampen the edges and fold down over the pastry base inside the edge of the flan tin. Cut a steam vent in the centre. Brush the pastry well with beaten egg. Bake in a moderate oven (375°F, 190°C, Gas Mark 5) for 30 minutes. Brush tourte with remaining egg and return to the oven for a further 10 minutes.

Apple snow

INGREDIENTS	METRIC	IMP.	U.S.
Cooking [baking] apples	450 g	1 lb	1 lb
4 tbspns water			
1 tspn ground cinnamon			
Little sugar			
2 egg whites			

Peel, core and slice the apples and stew with the water until soft. Beat to a smooth purée with the cinnamon. Sweeten to taste and cool. Stiffly whisk the egg whites, fold into the apple mixture and pour into a glass dish.

MENU

4

Orange-basted chicken with baby beetroots
Quick scalloped cauliflower
Caramel snow eggs

Orange-basted chicken with baby beetroots

INGREDIENTS	METRIC	IMP.	U.S.
1 chicken	1.5 kg	3 lb	3 lb
Salt and pepper			
2 tbspns frozen orange concentrate			
1 tbspn soy sauce			
2 tbspns boiling water			
Baby beetroots [beets]	450 g	1 lb	1 lb
BÉCHAMEL SAUCE			
1 small carrot			
1 small onion			
Milk	600 ml	1 pint	$2\frac{1}{2}$ cups
2 peppercorns			
1 bay leaf			
Pinch ground mace			
Butter	50 g	2 oz	$\frac{1}{4}$ cup
Flour	50 g	2 oz	$\frac{1}{2}$ cup
Salt and pepper			

Sprinkle the chicken with salt and pepper and place in a small roasting tin. Mix together the orange juice concentrate, soy sauce and boiling water. Roast the chicken in a moderately hot oven (400°F, 200°C, Gas Mark 6) for 1 hour and 20 minutes, basting frequently with the orange soy sauce after the first 20 minutes. Meanwhile, cook the beetroots and make the béchamel sauce. Trim the beetroots and cook in boiling salted water for about 20 minutes, until tender. To make the sauce, roughly chop the carrot and onion and place in a saucepan with the milk, peppercorns, bay leaf and mace. Bring to the boil and allow to stand for 10 minutes. In a clean saucepan melt the butter, stir in the flour and cook for 3 minutes without browning. Gradually strain in the flavoured milk and bring to the boil, stirring all the time, until the sauce is smooth and thick. Season to taste with salt and pepper. Place the chicken on a hot serving dish. Peel the beetroots, place them in a hot vegetable dish and pour the sauce over them.

Quick scalloped cauliflower

INGREDIENTS	METRIC	IMP.	U.S.
1 small cauliflower			
2 medium carrots			
Can condensed cream of mushroom soup	156 g	$5\frac{1}{2}$ oz	$5\frac{1}{2}$ oz
2 slices streaky [side] bacon			
Grated Cheddar cheese	50 g	2 oz	$\frac{1}{4}$ cup

Divide the cauliflower into florets. Cut the carrots into narrow strips. Cook vegetables in boiling salted water for 10 minutes. Drain, place in an ovenproof casserole dish. Pour the condensed soup over the vegetables. Fry the bacon until crisp. Drain and crumble. Sprinkle the cooked crumbled bacon and the grated cheese over the soup and vegetables. Bake in a moderate oven (350°F, 180°C, Gas Mark 4) for 20 minutes.

Another orange flavoured sauce for chicken is very quick to make, combining frozen orange concentrate with a purée of canned apricots. Dilute 2 tablespoons of concentrate with the same quantity of water and stir in 6 tablespoons sieved canned apricots. Sharpen the taste with a tablespoon of vinegar, a pinch of ground cinnamon and season generously with salt and pepper. Heat and serve with roast chicken, or oven-baked chicken portions on a bed of rice, and sprinkle the dish with paprika. If you like the sweet flavour, baste the chicken while it is cooking with apricot syrup.

Caramel snow eggs

INGREDIENTS	METRIC	IMP.	U.S.
3 eggs, separated			
Castor [granulated] sugar	50 g	2 oz	4 tbspns
Milk	600 ml	1 pint	2½ cups
Flaked [slivered] almonds	25 g	1 oz	¼ cup
CARAMEL			
Granulated sugar	100 g	4 oz	½ cup
Water	50 ml	2 fl oz	4 tbspns

Beat together the egg yolks, castor sugar and milk. Cook in a double boiler or over a very low heat in a pan with a heavy base, stirring gently, until a custard forms which coats the back of the spoon. Pour into a shallow serving dish and cool. Meanwhile, beat the egg whites until very stiff, and poach spoonfuls in simmering water until firm. Remove with a slotted draining spoon and place on top of the set custard. Sprinkle over the almonds. To make the caramel dissolve the granulated sugar in the water, over low heat, then boil until it turns colour. When golden brown, pour over the almonds.

23

MENU

5

Turkey and apricot pilau
Salade aux chapons
Cider and sultana sponge pudding

Turkey and apricot pilau

INGREDIENTS	METRIC	IMP.	U.S.
1 tbspn oil			
1 clove garlic, crushed			
1 onion, chopped			
Salt and pepper			
Pinch ground ginger			
Long grain rice	225 g	8 oz	½ lb
Cooked turkey	450 g	1 lb	1 lb
Chicken stock [broth]	600 ml	1 pint	2½ cups
Seedless raisins	50 g	2 oz	½ cup
Apricots	225 g	8 oz	½ lb
1 tbspn soy sauce			
1 tspn sherry			

Heat the oil and use to fry the garlic and onion until soft. Add salt, pepper, ground ginger and rice and fry quickly. Cut the turkey into cubes and add to the pan with the stock and raisins. Lower heat to simmer, cover and cook for 10 minutes. Halve the apricots, remove the stones and simmer in a little boiling water until just tender. Drain the apricots, add to the rice and continue cooking for a further 5 minutes. Stir in the soy sauce and sherry. Serve with a salad.

Salade aux chapons

INGREDIENTS	METRIC	IMP.	U.S.
2 large slices stale white bread, trimmed			
1 clove garlic			
4 tbspns French [Italian] dressing			
1 lettuce			
½ cucumber			
4 spring onions [scallions]			
1 tbspn chopped parsley			

Cut the bread into very small dice and fry golden brown all over in hot oil. Drain well and cool. Rub the salad bowl with the cut clove of garlic, or crush it and marinate in the salad dressing for at least 2 hours. Shred the lettuce, slice the cucumber and spring onions. Toss together the lettuce, cucumber, onion, parsley and chapons in the dressing and serve immediately.

Cider and sultana sponge pudding

INGREDIENTS	METRIC	IMP.	U.S.
TOPPING			
Medium sweet cider	150 ml	¼ pint	½ cup+
Sultanas [seedless white raisins]	100 g	4 oz	1 cup
Butter	25 g	1 oz	2 tbspns
2 tbspns golden [corn] syrup			
SPONGE			
Butter	50 g	2 oz	¼ cup
Castor [granulated] sugar	100 g	4 oz	½ cup
1 egg			
Flour	175 g	6 oz	1½ cups
2 rounded tspns baking powder			
Pinch of salt			
CIDER SAUCE			
Medium sweet cider	300 ml	½ pint	1¼ cups
1 tbspn golden [corn] syrup			
2 tspns cornflour [cornstarch]			

First make the topping. Pour the cider over the sultanas, leave to soak overnight, then drain and reserve liquid. Melt the butter and syrup in a small pan and heat until it begins to turn a caramel colour. Pour at once into a greased 7 inch/17.5 cm cake tin and arrange the soaked sultanas evenly on top. To make the sponge, cream the butter and sugar and gradually beat in the egg. Sieve the flour with the baking powder and salt and fold in with the reserved liquid. If necessary add further cider to give a soft dropping consistency. Spoon into the cake tin without disturbing the topping and leave a hollow in the centre. Bake in the centre of a moderate oven (350°F, 180°C, Gas Mark 4) for 50-55 minutes. Turn out at once on a heated dish. Meanwhile, make the sauce. Heat most of the cider with the syrup in a pan. Moisten the cornflour with the remaining cider, add to the pan and bring to the boil, stirring constantly. Simmer for 3 minutes and hand separately with the pudding.

Southern fried chicken
with concasse of tomatoes
Ribbon noodles
Courgettes and mushrooms
Rhubarb and mandarin tart

Southern fried chicken with concasse of tomatoes

INGREDIENTS	METRIC	IMP.	U.S.
4 southern fried chicken portions, defrosted			
Oil for frying			
Ribbon noodles	225 g	8 oz	$\frac{1}{2}$ lb
Butter	75 g	3 oz	6 tbspns
Salt and pepper			
Button mushrooms	225 g	8 oz	$\frac{1}{2}$ lb
2 tspns lemon juice			
Courgettes [zucchini]	225 g	8 oz	$\frac{1}{2}$ lb
1 tbspn oil			
CONCASSE			
Tomatoes	450 g	1 lb	1 lb
1 small onion, grated			
2 tbspns oil			
1 tbspn vinegar			
1 tspn ground nutmeg			
1 tspn sugar			
Salt and ground black pepper			

Deep fry the chicken joints in hot oil as instructions on the pack. Cook the noodles in boiling salted water for about 12 minutes, until just tender. Rinse in hot water and toss with 1 oz/ 25 g of the butter, salt and pepper to taste. Sprinkle the mushrooms with lemon juice and slice the courgettes. Heat together the remaining butter and the oil and use to fry the mushrooms and courgettes until light brown. Meanwhile, make the concasse. Skin the tomatoes, remove seeds and chop the flesh. Mix with all other ingredients and place in a saucepan. Bring to the boil and simmer until the sauce thickens slightly. Arrange chicken portions on a bed of noodles, place the courgettes and mushrooms round the chicken and pour over the concasse of tomatoes.

Double crust fruit pies and tarts can be made much more interesting if two fruits are combined in the filling. Both strawberries and raspberries combine well with rhubarb, cherries with apple, and blackcurrants or blackberries with either apple or pear. To ensure that the juices do not run out of the pastry, sprinkle with sugar for sweetening and a little cornflour (cornstarch) to thicken the juice. Some very juicy fruits make the bottom layer of pastry soggy. It is a useful trick to separate the egg used for glazing, lightly beat the white and brush inside the bottom layer of pastry to seal it before placing fruit on top. In this case add sufficient water to the yolk to make an egg wash to glaze the top of the pie or tart and the trimmings. Leaves are the most popular form of trimming and they are easy to make if a thinly rolled strip of pastry about 1 inch/2.5 cm wide is sliced through diagonally at regular intervals then marked with the tip of a knife to show the veins and pinched up to indicate the 'stem' end.

Rhubarb and mandarin tart

INGREDIENTS	METRIC	IMP.	U.S.
Plain [all-purpose] flour	350 g	12 oz	3 cups
½ tspn salt			
White vegetable cooking fat	175 g	6 oz	⅔ cup
3 tbspns cold water			
FILLING			
Canned unsweetened mandarin oranges	300 g	11 oz	11 oz
Rhubarb	225g	8 oz	½ lb
3 tbspns clear honey			
1 tspn cornflour [cornstarch]			
1 egg, beaten			

Place the flour, salt, fat and water in a bowl, crumbling up the fat with a strong fork. Mix with the fork until a firm ball of dough is formed. Knead lightly on a floured board, roll out thinly and divide into two pieces, one slightly larger than the other. Use the larger piece to line an 8 inch/20 cm pie plate, and keep the smaller piece for the lid. To make the filling, drain the mandarin oranges, reserving the juice. Cut the rhubarb into short lengths. Arrange rhubarb and mandarin segments in the pastry case and trickle the honey over the fruit. Sieve the cornflour on top and cover with the pastry lid. Dampen edges, seal well together and cut a steam vent. Use pastry trimmings to decorate the pie. Brush with beaten egg and bake in a hot oven (425°F, 220°C, Gas Mark 7) for 15 minutes, then reduce heat slightly for a further 20 minutes, or until golden brown.
Note: Use the juice from the mandarins instead of water to stew rhubarb, sweetened with honey, for another occasion.

27

Sole with spiced butter
Asparagus with Orange hollandaise sauce
Gooseberry fool with ice cream

Sole with spiced butter

INGREDIENTS	METRIC	IMP.	U.S.
Clarified butter	100 g	4 oz	½ cup
1 tbspn oil			
Salt and pepper			
Fillets of sole	225 g	8 oz	½ lb
5 tspns lemon juice			
Chopped parsley	25 g	1 oz	2 tbspns
2 spring [green] onions, chopped			
1 tspn herb and spice blend for fish			
Lemon wedges			
Parsley sprigs			

Melt butter and oil together in a wide heavy frying pan. Season the fillets if required and sauté them over a high heat for 2-3 minutes on each side until golden brown. Transfer to a serving dish, sprinkle with lemon juice and keep hot. Add parsley, spring onion and spices to the pan and cook until butter turns brown but not burnt. Pour over fish and serve garnished with lemon wedges and parsley sprigs. Serves 2.

Gooseberry fool with ice cream

INGREDIENTS	METRIC	IMP.	U.S.
Gooseberries	225 g	8 oz	½ lb
2 tbspns water			
Sugar			
1 tbspn cornflour [cornstarch]			
Milk	150 ml	¼ pint	½ cup
Few drops vanilla essence [extract]			
Few drops green food colouring			
1 gingernut biscuit			
1 piece preserved ginger			
2 scoops vanilla ice cream			

Cook the gooseberries with the water and sugar to taste until soft. Sieve, or liquidize and then sieve, to remove the skins and pips. Moisten the cornflour with 2 tablespoons of the milk. Heat the remaining milk, add the blended cornflour and bring to boiling point, stirring constantly. Simmer for 3 minutes. Add sugar to taste and a few drops of vanilla essence. Beat in the gooseberry purée and colour pale green with a drop or two of food colouring if liked. Cool. Crumble the gingernut biscuit and chop the piece of ginger. Divide the mixture between two glass serving dishes, top each with a scoop of ice cream and decorate the top with pieces of gingernut and ginger. Serve with additional gingernut biscuits. Serves 2.

Orange hollandaise sauce for asparagus

INGREDIENTS	METRIC	IMP.	U.S.
2 egg yolks			
Salt and pepper			
1 tbspn lemon juice			
Orange juice	2 tbspns	2 tbspns	3 tbspns
1 tspn vinegar			
Butter	100 g	4 oz	½ cup
Single cream [half & half]	2 tbspns	2 tbspns	3 tbspns

Put the egg yolks, seasoning to taste, lemon juice, orange juice and vinegar into a double saucepan, or basin over a pan of simmering water. Whisk until the sauce begins to thicken. Add the butter in small pieces, whisking each one in until completely melted before adding another. Do not allow the sauce to boil, and if it becomes too thick, whisk in the cream. Serve with fresh asparagus boiled in salted water for 15 minutes.

Chicken and chips in a basket
Radish salad
Plum flan with raisin sauce

Chicken and chips in a basket

INGREDIENTS	METRIC	IMP.	U.S.
4 1 lb/450 g spring chickens			
Salt and pepper			
Butter	100 g	4 oz	$\frac{1}{2}$ cup
Small bunch parsley			
Potatoes	700 g	$1\frac{1}{2}$ lb	$1\frac{1}{2}$ lb
Oil for frying			
2 bunches watercress			

Serving baskets should each be lined with a square of foil before the paper napkin is put in place. This prevents oil seeping through the paper and marking the wickerwork. If you have no small baskets, individual wooden salad bowls can be used instead. As it is usual to eat such tiny chickens with the fingers be sure to have plenty more paper napkins available.

Season inside the carcase of each chicken with salt and pepper and insert a small knob of butter and a sprig of parsley. Melt the remaining butter and use to brush the skins. Roast in a moderately hot oven (400°F, 200°C, Gas Mark 6) for 40-45 minutes, until golden brown. Use a trivet in a roasting pan to ensure even browning. Meanwhile, cut the potatoes into matchstick size chips. Soak in iced water for 30 minutes. Drain and dry. Heat the oil until hot but not smoking (about 225°F, 132°C). Place the chips in a frying basket and plunge into the hot oil. Fry until soft. Remove basket, shake dry and raise the temperature of the oil to smoking hot. Add the chips for a few seconds until golden brown. Drain well and keep hot. Fold four white paper napkins and place one in the bottom of each basket. Divide the chips between the baskets and place the roast chickens on top. Surround with sprigs of watercress.

Plum flan with raisin sauce

INGREDIENTS	METRIC	IMP.	U.S.
Butter	75 g	3 oz	6 tbspns
Castor [granulated] sugar	75 g	3 oz	6 tbspns
2 eggs			
½ tspn vanilla essence [extract]			
Flour	75 g	3 oz	¾ cup
Seedless raisins	50 g	2 oz	⅓ cup
2 tbspns rum			
4-5 large yellow or red plums			
4 tbspns apricot jam			
Glacé [candied] cherries			

Cream the butter and sugar until light and fluffy and gradually beat in the eggs and vanilla essence. Fold in the flour and place the mixture in an 8 inch/20 cm flan tin. Bake in a moderately hot oven (375°F, 190°C, Gas Mark 5) for 25-30 minutes. Cool on a wire rack. Meanwhile, soak the raisins in the rum. Halve and stone the plums. Heat the jam and sieve it. Mix with the raisins and rum. Place the plums, cut side down, in the flan case, pour over the raisin mixture and decorate with glacé cherries.

MENU

9

Oysters with croquettes
Crisp celery salad
Zabaglione

Oysters with croquettes

INGREDIENTS	METRIC	IMP.	U.S.
1 egg, beaten			
Mashed potato	*450 g*	*1 lb*	*1 lb*
Little milk			
Salt and pepper			
Peeled shrimps	*100 g*	*4 oz*	*¾ cup*
Grated Gruyère [Swiss] cheese	*50 g*	*2 oz*	*½ cup*
Seasoned flour for coating			
Oil for frying			
16 oysters			

Beat the egg into the mashed potato with a little milk, if necessary, to make a very thick purée. Season to taste. Finely chop the shrimps and fold into the potato mixture with the cheese. Chill and shape into small croquettes with floured hands. Coat with seasoned flour and deep fry in hot oil until golden brown, about 4 minutes. Arrange croquettes on a platter surrounding the oysters.

Crisp celery salad

INGREDIENTS	METRIC	IMP.	U.S.
1 large head celery			
Cooked green peas	225 g	8 oz	½ lb
6 spring onions [scallions] chopped			
DRESSING			
½ tspn salt			
¼ tspn pepper			
¼ tspn prepared mustard			
Finely grated rind and juice of 1 lime or lemon			
5 tbspns oil			
Sprig of watercress to garnish			

Trim any damaged leaves off the celery, and use for stew or soup. Slice the rest of the celery obliquely into 1 inch/2 cm lengths. To make the dressing, mix together the salt, pepper, mustard, lime rind and juice. Beat in the oil gradually. Use to toss the vegetables and pile up in a salad bowl. Garnish with a sprig of watercress.

Zabaglione

INGREDIENTS	METRIC	IMP.	U.S.
4 egg yolks			
Castor [granulated] sugar	50 g	2 oz	4 tbspns
4 tbspns Marsala			
Few chopped almonds or hazelnuts			

Put the egg yolks, sugar and Marsala in a non-stick saucepan or double boiler. Beat until thick and creamy. Place saucepan over very low heat and continue beating until mixture becomes pale and at least doubles its bulk. Remove from heat occasionally and scrape the bottom gently with a plastic spatula. Continue beating until the mixture forms a stiff peak and adheres to the beaters when they are lifted out. Spoon gently into glasses and sprinkle lightly with chopped almonds or hazelnuts. Serve warm.

MENU

10

Aubergines in cream cheese
Herring potato balls with dill
Loganberry ice cream

Aubergines in cream cheese

INGREDIENTS	METRIC	IMP.	U.S.
4 medium aubergines [eggplants]			
Salt and ground black pepper			
6 tbspns oil			
Cream cheese	175 g	6 oz	6 oz
Single cream [half & half]	150 ml	$\frac{1}{4}$ pint	$\frac{1}{2}$ cup
1 clove garlic, chopped			
2 tbspns finely chopped chives			

Peel the aubergines, cut in slices lengthwise, sprinkle with salt and leave to stand for 30 minutes. Rinse and dry with absorbent kitchen paper. Cook until pale golden in the oil, remove, draining them carefully, and keep hot. Beat together the cream cheese, cream, garlic, chives and freshly ground pepper to taste. Use any surplus oil to grease a shallow flameproof dish. Fill with alternate layers of aubergine and cheese mixture, ending with a layer of cheese. Place under a medium grill until well browned.

Herring potato balls with dill

INGREDIENTS	METRIC	IMP.	U.S.
Potatoes	450 g	1 lb	1 lb
1 egg			
1 tspn dill seed			
Salt and pepper			
Cooked herring	225 g	8 oz	$\frac{1}{2}$ lb
Dry breadcrumbs			
Oil for frying			

Cook the potatoes in boiling salted water until tender. Mash, then beat in the egg, dill seed, salt and pepper. Cut the cooked herring into 24 small pieces. Shape the mashed potatoes into small balls, pressing a piece of herring into the middle of each ball. Roll the potato balls in dry breadcrumbs. Fry in hot deep oil until lightly browned. Drain and spear on cocktail sticks. Serve hot.

Drained sardines may be substituted for the herring.

Loganberry ice cream

INGREDIENTS	METRIC	IMP.	U.S.
Creamy milk	300 ml	$\frac{1}{2}$ pint	$1\frac{1}{4}$ cups
2 eggs, separated			
Castor [granulated] sugar	75 g	3 oz	6 tbspns
1 vanilla pod [bean]			
Loganberry purée	250 ml	8 fl oz	1 cup
Double [whipping] cream	450 ml	$\frac{3}{4}$ pint	2 cups

Put the milk, egg yolks, sugar and vanilla pod in a bowl and place over a pan of hot water. Cook over the heat until the custard thickens sufficiently to coat the back of a spoon. Remove from the heat, discard the vanilla pod and leave the custard to cool. When cold, stir in the fruit purée. Fold in the fairly stiffly whipped cream and stiffly beaten egg whites. Place the mixture in a clean bowl, cover lightly with freezer film and place in the freezer until the mixture is partially frozen. Take out and beat the mixture until it is smooth then transfer to a suitable container. Freeze. Serve in small glass dishes.
Note: To make a fruit and nut ice cream, add 4 oz/100 g/$\frac{3}{4}$ cup chopped hazelnuts or almonds.

34

MENU

11

Artichoke omelette

Rhubarb and orange fool

Artichoke omelette

INGREDIENTS	METRIC	IMP.	U.S.
6 cooked Globe artichoke bottoms			
8 eggs			
Salt and pepper			
Milk	4 tbspns	4 tbspns	⅓ cup
Butter	15 g	½ oz	1 tbspn
1 tbspn chopped chives			

Cut the artichoke bottoms in half. Beat together the eggs with the salt and pepper to taste and the milk, until foamy. In a big frying pan melt the butter and toss the artichoke bottoms in it over moderate heat for 2 minutes. Pour in the eggs and cook, shaking the pan and allowing surplus egg to run under the edges until lightly set but still very moist in the centre. Sprinkle over the chopped chives and serve cut in wedges.

Rhubarb and orange fool

INGREDIENTS	METRIC	IMP.	U.S.
1 orange			
Trimmed rhubarb	450 g	1 lb	1 lb
Sugar	75 g	3 oz	6 tbspns
Custard [vanilla sauce]	150 ml	¼ pint	½ cup +
Double [whipping] cream, whipped	150 ml	¼ pint	½ cup

Grate the rind from the orange and squeeze the juice. Cut the rhubarb into short lengths and cook gently with the orange juice and rind, the sugar and just sufficient water to cover. Cool, and sieve or liquidise in a blender. Stir in the custard, then the cream and pour into a glass serving dish. Chill.

MENU

12

Cheesey Charlies with Spiced cherry sauce
Lettuce and cucumber salad

Cheesey Charlies

INGREDIENTS	METRIC	IMP.	U.S.
Shredded [chopped beef] suet	50 g	2 oz	½ cup
Water	150 ml	¼ pint	½ cup
Flour	50 g	2 oz	½ cup
2 eggs, beaten			
Grated cheese	50 g	2 oz	½ cup
Salt and cayenne pepper			
Pinch dry mustard			
Oil for frying			

Melt the suet in a saucepan, add water and bring to the boil. Add the flour and beat thoroughly with a wooden spoon until the mixture forms a ball and leaves the sides of the pan clean. Remove from the heat, cool slightly and gradually beat in the eggs, then beat in the cheese and seasonings. Drop teaspoonfuls of the mixture into hot oil or fat and deep fry for about 5 minutes until golden brown. Drain on absorbent paper and serve hot, with the following sauce:

Spiced cherry sauce

INGREDIENTS	METRIC	IMP.	U.S.
Tart cherries	4 oz	1 lb	1 lb
White vinegar	100 ml	3 fl oz	⅓ cup
½ tspn ground allspice			
Soft [light] brown sugar	100 g	4 oz	½ cup
2 tspns cornflour [cornstarch]			

Stone the cherries. Place in a saucepan with the vinegar and allspice and bring to the boil. Cover, reduce heat and simmer gently for 15 minutes. Stir in the sugar until dissolved, return to the boil, cover, reduce heat and simmer for a further 10 minutes. Moisten the cornflour with a little cold water, stir into the pan and cook until thickened and clear, stirring constantly. Hand separately in a sauceboat.

MENU

13

Beef stew with apricot dumplings
French beans
Grape and coconut flan

Beef stew with apricot dumplings

INGREDIENTS	METRIC	IMP.	U.S.
Stewing steak	450 g	1 lb	1 lb
Apricots	350 g	12 oz	¾ lb
Butter	40 g	1½ oz	3 tbspns
Button onions	225 g	8 oz	½ lb
1 beef stock [bouillon] cube			
Few drops gravy browning			
1 tbspn cornflour [cornstarch]			
Salt and pepper			
DUMPLINGS			
Self-raising flour [all-purpose flour + 1½ tspns baking powder]	175 g	6 oz	1½ cups
Shredded [chopped beef] suet	75 g	3 oz	½ cup
Salt and pepper			
Water to mix			

Dice and trim the meat neatly. Stone and halve the apricots. Reserve 6 halves for the dumplings and chop these finely. Melt the butter and use to sauté the meat and onions until golden. Dissolve the stock cube in ¾ pint/450 ml/2 cups boiling water and add sufficient gravy browning to colour well. Add the apricot halves to the pan, cook for a further 30 seconds and pour over the stock. Cover and simmer for about 1½ hours, until the meat is tender. Meanwhile, make up the dumpling mixture with the reserved apricots and just sufficient water to make a soft dough. Form into about 8 dumplings with floured hands and cook in boiling salted water for 15 minutes. Taste the stew and adjust seasoning. Moisten the cornflour with a little cold water, stir into the pan and bring back to the boil, stirring constantly. Drain the dumplings and add to the stew.

Unusual dumplings add interest to stews. Dried fruit, including apricots, apple rings and prunes cut into small pieces, seedless raisins and currants can all be used without pre-soaking. Most dried sweet herbs add appeal to dumplings as does grated stale hard cheese. Spices can be combined with grated orange or lemon rind for an exotic touch.

Grape and coconut flan

INGREDIENTS	METRIC	IMP.	U.S.
3 eggs			
Castor [granulated] sugar	75 g	3 oz	$\frac{1}{3}$ cup
Plain [all-purpose] flour	75 g	3 oz	$\frac{3}{4}$ cup
Butter, melted	25 g	1 oz	2 tbspns
FILLING			
4 tbspns grated fresh coconut			
Apricot jam	225 g	8 oz	$\frac{1}{2}$ cup
Green grapes	75 g	3 oz	$\frac{1}{2}$ cup
Black [Tokay] grapes	75 g	3 oz	$\frac{1}{2}$ cup
Grated fresh coconut to decorate			

To make the flan case, whisk the eggs and sugar together over a bowl of hot water until thick and the whisk leaves a trail when lifted from the mixture. Remove from the heat and continue whisking until cold. Fold in the flour and butter until well blended. Turn mixture into a greased 8 inch/20 cm flan tin and bake in a moderately hot oven (375°F, 190°C, Gas Mark 5) for 20 minutes. Cool on a wire rack. To make the filling, mix the coconut with three-quarters of the jam and spread in the base of the flan case. Halve the grapes and remove the pips. Fill the flan case decoratively with the halved grapes. Sieve the remaining apricot jam and heat in a small pan with 1 tablespoon water. Use this glaze to brush over the grapes and decorate the top with a little more grated coconut.

Roast lamb with lemon chutney sauce
Minted new potatoes and peas
Greengage strudel

Roast lamb with lemon chutney sauce

INGREDIENTS	METRIC	IMP.	U.S.
Leg of lamb	2¼ kg.	4½ lb	4½ lb
Salt and pepper			
New potatoes	700 g	1½ lb	1½ lb
SAUCE			
1 beef stock [bouillon] cube			
1 small onion			
Lard	40 g	1½ oz	3 tbspns
Flour	25 g	1 oz	¼ cup
Red wine	150 ml	¼ pint	⅔ cup
2 tbspns mango chutney			
Juice of ½ lemon			
Pared rind of 1 lemon			
Few sprigs parsley			

Season the leg with salt and pepper and place in a roasting tin. Roast in a moderately hot oven (400°F, 200°C, Gas Mark 6) for 20 minutes per lb/450 g plus 20 minutes over. Meanwhile cook the potatoes in boiling salted water until tender. Remove the joint and keep hot. Make a stock with the pan juices, ½ pint/300 ml/1¼ cups boiling water and the stock cube. Finely chop the onion. Melt the lard and use to cook the onion over low heat until light golden. Stir in the flour and cook together until pale brown. Remove from the heat and gradually add the stock. Bring to the boil, stirring constantly, and cook for 2 minutes. Strain and add the wine, chutney, lemon juice and rind. Return to the pan and reheat but do not boil. Adjust seasoning and pour into a sauce boat. Serve the joint with potatoes and peas. Hand the sauce separately. Serves 6.

Flaky pastry is an alternative to the sweet strudel pastry given here. Sift 225 g/8 oz/ 2 cups plain (all-purpose) flour and ½ teaspoon salt into a bowl. Divide 150 g/ 5 oz/⅔ cup whipped white vegetable fat into four portions and rub one into the flour mixture. Add 150 ml/¼ pint/generous ½ cup water and mix to a soft dough with a round-bladed knife. Turn out on a floured surface and roll out to a rectangle about 30 cm/12 inches by 15 cm/ 6 inches. Using a further one quarter of the fat, dot small pieces over two-thirds of the pastry. Fold the uncovered third of the pastry up over the middle third and fold the top third down. Seal the edges and give the pastry a one-quarter turn. Allow it to rest for 15 minutes. Repeat the rolling, dotting, folding and resting processes twice more. This makes 450 g/1 lb of pastry. It is useful for covering deep-dish fruit pies, making strudels and other attractive sweet pastry dishes such as 'Beehive' apples where long strips of the pastry are wound round baking apples to cover them completely. They are then glazed with egg and baked in the oven until golden brown like apple dumplings.

Greengage strudel

INGREDIENTS	METRIC	IMP.	U.S.
Greengages [greengage plums]	1 kg	2 lb	2 lb
Ground almonds	75 g	3 oz	⅔ cup
Castor [granulated] sugar	40 g	1½ oz	3 tbspns
PASTRY			
Flour	350 g	12 oz	3 cups
Pinch of salt			
2 tbspns castor [granulated] sugar			
Butter	100 g	4 oz	½ cup
Scant 2 tbspns water			
Little milk for brushing			

Halve the greengages and remove the stones. Mix together the ground almonds and sugar and sprinkle over the fruit. To make the pastry, sieve the flour with the salt and stir in the sugar. Rub in the butter and add just enough water to make a firm paste. Chill for 30 minutes then roll out thinly into a rectangle. Cover the centre with the fruit, fold in the sides, dampen and press firmly to make a roll. Seal the ends, turn over and place on a buttered baking sheet. Brush with milk and bake in a moderate oven (350°F, 180°C, Gas Mark 4) for 35-40 minutes, until golden brown. Serve warm with cream. Serves 6.

MENU

15

Scallop mélange au gratin
Fluffy boiled rice with dill weed
Blackberry and pear pudding

Scallop mélange au gratin

INGREDIENTS	METRIC	IMP.	U.S.
4 large scallops			
Water	300 ml	½ pint	1¼ cups
Dry white wine	150 ml	¼ pint	½ cup
Slice of onion			
1 bay leaf			
½ tspn salt			
2 peppercorns			
1 medium carrot, peeled			
1 stalk celery			
4 large Brussels sprouts			
2 tbspns butter or margarine			
Salt and pepper			
SAUCE			
1 tbspn butter			
1 tbspn flour			
Milk	150 ml	¼ pint	⅔ cup
Grated Cheddar cheese	25 g	1 oz	¼ cup

Clean the scallops. Combine the water, white wine, onion, bay leaf, salt and peppercorns, in a small saucepan. Add the scallops, bring to the boil and simmer for 5 minutes. Finely dice the carrot and celery. Wash and slice the Brussels sprouts. Sauté the vegetables in the butter until soft. Season with salt and pepper. Place a small amount of the vegetables in individual oven-proof dishes or scallop shells. Drain and slice the scallops. Arrange on top of the vegetables. Make a cheese sauce by melting the butter in a small saucepan. Stir in the flour, gradually add the milk and cook until thickened, stirring constantly. Add the grated cheese. Season to taste with salt and pepper. Pour over the scallop and vegetable mixture. Brown under a hot grill. Serve with boiled rice flavoured with dill.

Blackberry and pear pudding

INGREDIENTS	METRIC	IMP.	U.S.
Plain [all-purpose] flour	225 g	8 oz	2 cups
½ tspn salt			
1 tspn sugar			
Milk	125 ml	4 fl oz	½ cup
1 tspn dried yeast			
Butter	50 g	2 oz	¼ cup
2 eggs			
3 medium pears			
1 tbspn castor [granulated] sugar			
Blackberries	225 g	8 oz	½ lb

Sieve the flour and salt together into a bowl. Dissolve the sugar in the warm milk and sprinkle the dried yeast on top. Leave for about 10 minutes, or until frothy. Melt the butter and beat the yeast mixture into the flour, work in the melted butter and the lightly beaten eggs to give a soft dough. Allow to rise, covered, in a warm place until doubled in bulk. Meanwhile, peel, quarter and core the pears, and roll in the castor sugar. Butter a loose-bottomed 8 inch/20 cm cake tin or deep flan tin; knock back the risen dough and shape to fit the tin, leaving a raised edge. Fill the centre with the pears. Bake in a moderately hot oven (375°F, 190°C, Gas Mark 5) for 30-40 minutes. Test that the dough is cooked by inserting the blade of a knife which should come out clean. Remove from the oven, unmould, and sprinkle with the blackberries.

MENU

16

Spanish tortilla omelette
Peach toasts

Spanish tortilla omelette

INGREDIENTS	METRIC	IMP.	U.S.
Large potatoes	*500 g*	*1 lb*	*1 lb*
1 large onion			
Stuffed green olives	*75 g*	*3 oz*	*½ cup*
Olive oil	*75 ml*	*3 fl oz*	*⅓ cup*
1½ tspns salt			
4 eggs			
Ground black pepper			

Cut the potatoes into very thin slices, finely chop the onion and slice the olives. Heat the oil in a large heavy pan, add the potatoes and 1 teaspoon of salt. Stir to coat with oil and cook over moderate heat for about 10 minutes. Stir in the onion and cook for a further 10 minutes until the potatoes are tender and becoming golden brown. Drain off oil. Add the olives to the potato mixture. In a large basin, whisk the eggs with the remaining salt and the black pepper until blended. Add the potato mixture to the eggs. Heat about 2 tablespoons more oil in a large frying pan, pour in the omelette mixture and spread out evenly. Allow to cook over moderate heat until set and browned underneath. Place a plate on top of the pan, turn pan over so that the omelette turns out on to the plate. Carefully slide omelette back into the pan, browned side up, and cook for a further 2-3 minutes to brown the underside. Serve immediately cut into quarters.

Peach toasts

INGREDIENTS	METRIC	IMP.	U.S.
4 large slices white bread			
4 slices ham			
2 ripe peaches			
4 thin slices Gouda [Dutch] cheese			
Cayenne pepper			

Remove crusts if liked, and toast the bread lightly. Place a slice of ham, trimmed to fit, on each piece of toast. Arrange wedges of freshly peeled and stoned peaches on this. Cover with thin slices of Gouda cheese, also trimmed to fit, sprinkle with cayenne pepper and place under a hot grill until the cheese begins to melt and bubble. Serve at once with a fresh green salad, or a bowl of watercress sprigs.

45

Fish in capered mayonnaise
Pan chicken and vegetables
Mixed salad
Coffee and nut ice cream

Fish in capered mayonnaise

INGREDIENTS	METRIC	IMP.	U.S.
Hake or halibut, steamed	350 g	12 oz	$\frac{3}{4}$ lb
Juice of $\frac{1}{2}$ lemon			
Salt and freshly ground black pepper			
1 clove garlic, crushed			
1 tbspn capers			
Mayonnaise	150 ml	$\frac{1}{4}$ pint	$\frac{1}{2}$ cup
Double [whipping] cream	150 ml	$\frac{1}{4}$ pint	$\frac{1}{2}$ cup
Liquid aspic jelly	150 ml	$\frac{1}{4}$ pint	$\frac{1}{2}$ cup

Skin and flake the fish. Season the lemon juice lightly with salt and pepper and use to toss the fish. Fold the garlic and capers into the mayonnaise. Whip the cream until thick but not stiff, fold in first the mayonnaise, then the aspic jelly when it is syrupy. Combine with the fish and spoon the mixture on to a serving platter. Serve chilled, garnished with parsley sprigs.

Pan chicken and vegetables

INGREDIENTS	METRIC	IMP.	U.S.
4 chicken breasts			
8 small carrots			
8 small courgettes [zucchini]			
Chicken stock [broth]	375 ml	12 fl oz	$1\frac{1}{2}$ cups
Dry white wine	250 ml	8 fl oz	1 cup
3 tbspns grated onion			
1 bay leaf			
$\frac{1}{4}$ tspn dried [crushed] rosemary			
2 tbspns cornflour [cornstarch]			
3 tbspns chopped canned red pimiento			
2 tbspns chopped parsley			

Halve the chicken breasts and halve the carrots and courgettes lengthways. Combine the stock, wine, onion, bay leaf and rosemary in a large pan. Bring to boiling point and add the chicken breasts. Cover and simmer for 10 minutes. Add the carrots, cook for a further 10 minutes. Add the courgettes and cook 10 minutes more. Remove the chicken and vegetables with a slotted spoon and keep hot. Moisten the cornflour with 2 tablespoons cold water, stir into the liquid remaining in the pan. Bring to boiling point, stirring constantly. Add the pimiento and parsley. Return the chicken and vegetables to the pan and baste with the sauce.

Coffee and nut ice cream

INGREDIENTS	METRIC	IMP.	U.S.
2 eggs			
Sifted icing [confectioner's] sugar	4 tbspns	4 tbspns	5 tbspns
Coffee essence [strong black coffee]	2 tbspns	2 tbspns	3 tbspns
Double [whipping] cream	150 ml	$\frac{1}{4}$ pint	$\frac{2}{3}$ cup
Coarsely chopped walnuts or hazelnuts	50 g	2 oz	1 cup

Separate the eggs and whisk the whites until stiff. Fold in the sieved icing sugar. Whisk the egg yolks and coffee essence together. Combine the two egg mixtures, beating gently. Whip the cream until slightly thickened, then fold into the mixture together with the chopped nuts. Spoon the mixture into freezing trays, or a polythene container. Seal, label and freeze. Serve sprinkled with a few extra chopped nuts and chocolate sauce, if liked.

MENU

18

Beef and egg pies
Green salad
Vicarage trifle

Beef and egg pies

INGREDIENTS	METRIC	IMP.	U.S.
1 green pepper			
1 red pepper			
4 small or 2 medium onions			
4 stalks celery			
2 large tomatoes			
Courgettes [zucchini]	450 g	1 lb	1 lb
2 hard-boiled eggs			
Whipped white vegetable fat	25 g	1 oz	2 tbspns
Minced [ground] beef	450 g	1 lb	1 lb
SAUCE			
Whipped white vegetable fat	25 g	1 oz	2 tbspns
2 tbspns curry powder			
2 tbspns flour			
Apple juice	600 ml	1 pint	2½ cups
4 tbspns brown table sauce			
Salt			
Flaky pastry [paste]	450 g	1 lb	1 lb
Beaten egg			

Deseed and chop the peppers and chop the onions, celery and tomatoes. Slice the courgettes and quarter the eggs. Melt the fat and use to fry the onion, celery, courgettes and pepper for 5 minutes. Add the meat and cook gently, stirring, until it changes colour. Add the tomato, cover and cook gently for 10 minutes. Meanwhile, make the sauce. Melt the fat and stir in the curry powder. Fry gently for 2 minutes. Sprinkle in the flour and stir well, then gradually add the apple juice and bring to boiling point, stirring constantly. Blend in the brown sauce and add salt to taste. Divide the meat mixture between 2 pie dishes, pour over the curry sauce, top with egg quarters and cover with flaky pastry, sealing it well to the edges of the dish. Cut a steam vent and decorate the top with leaves made from the pastry trimmings. Brush with beaten egg and bake in a hot oven (425°F, 220°C, Gas Mark 7) for 35-40 minutes. Serves 8.

Note: See recipe for flaky pastry on page 41.

Vicarage trifle

INGREDIENTS	METRIC	IMP.	U.S.
2 large cooking [baking] apples			
Sugar	50 g	2 oz	$\frac{1}{4}$ cup
Thick sweetened custard [vanilla sauce]	300 ml	$\frac{1}{2}$ pint	$1\frac{1}{4}$ cups
Double [whipping] cream	300 ml	$\frac{1}{2}$ pint	$1\frac{1}{4}$ cups
1 red-skinned eating apple			
1 tbspn lemon juice			
2 tbspns breadcrumbs browned in butter			
2 tbspns demerara [brown] sugar			
Angelica			

Peel, core and slice the cooking apples, cook with a little water and the sugar until reduced to a purée. Whisk in the custard until smooth. Cool. Half-whip the cream and fold into the apple custard, reserving about one third for the decoration. Pour the apple mixture into a glass serving dish and chill. Core and slice the dessert apple without peeling and toss in the lemon juice to prevent discolouration. Whip the remaining cream until stiff. Toss the buttered crumbs and demerara sugar together and spread over the surface of the apple mixture. Surround the edge of the dish with apple slices, chop the remaining apple and sprinkle over the centre and decorate with rosettes of whipped cream and angelica 'diamonds'. Serves 8.

49

MENU

19

Mackerel with apple stuffing
Courgettes with black olives
Pancake soufflé

Mackerel with apple stuffing

INGREDIENTS	METRIC	IMP.	U.S.
2 medium mackerel			
1 small onion			
2 Bramley [baking] apples			
Butter	100 g	4 oz	½ cup
Bread cubes	75 g	3 oz	1 cup
Grated rind of ½ lemon			
1 tbspn chopped parsley			
Pinch dried basil			
Salt and pepper			
Parsley sprigs			

Clean the mackerel and remove the heads. Chop the onion and one of the apples. Fry the chopped onion and apple in half of the butter until soft. Add the bread cubes, lemon rind, herbs and seasoning. Use to stuff the mackerel and secure with skewers. Bake in a moderate oven (350°F, 180°C, Gas Mark 4) for 40 minutes or until golden brown and cooked through. Core and slice the remaining apple and fry in the remaining butter until golden, turning once. Overlap the apple slices along each side of the mackerel and garnish with the parsley sprigs. Serves 2.

Courgettes with black olives

INGREDIENTS	METRIC	IMP.	U.S.
Courgettes [zucchini]	450 g	1 lb	1 lb
2 tomatoes			
1 small onion			
1 tbspn oil			
Small black olives	25 g	1 oz	1 tbspn
½ tspn dried thyme			
1 bay leaf			
Salt and pepper			

Slice the courgettes, peel and chop tomatoes, and finely chop the onion. Heat the oil in a pan and use to cook the onion gently until soft but not brown. Add the courgettes, tomato, olives, thyme and bay leaf. Bring to the boil, cover and simmer for 25 minutes or until the courgettes are soft. Season to taste and remove the bay leaf. Serves 2.

Pancake soufflé

INGREDIENTS	METRIC	IMP.	U.S.
2 eggs			
½ tspn salt			
2 tbspns castor [granulated] sugar			
Plain [all-purpose] flour	65 g	2½ oz	⅔ cup
Milk	100 ml	4 fl oz	½ cup
1 tspn butter			
1 tbspn icing [confectioner's] sugar			

Separate the eggs and beat the yolks with the salt and one tablespoon of the sugar. Stir in the flour and the milk. Beat until smooth. Whisk the egg whites with the remaining tablespoon of sugar until soft peaks form. Fold the batter gently into the egg white meringue. Melt the butter in a shallow, ovenproof dish. Pour in the batter and cook over low heat for 2 minutes. Then place in a hot oven (450°F, 230°C, Gas Mark 8) for 10-15 minutes or until the surface is nicely browned. Sprinkle with the icing sugar while hot. Serve with thick cream and red fruit jam. Serves 2.

Pasta with pork stroganoff
Bel Paese cheese with French bread

Pasta with pork stroganoff

INGREDIENTS	METRIC	IMP.	U.S.
Pork fillet [tenderloin]	575 g	1¼ lb	1¼ lb
Butter	50 g	2 oz	¼ cup
Mushrooms, sliced	100 g	4 oz	1 cup
Onions, chopped	100 g	4 oz	¾ cup
1 tbspn flour			
Tomato purée [paste]	65 g	2½ oz	5 tbspns
1 tspn sugar			
Salt and pepper			
Soured cream	150 ml	¼ pint	½ cup
Elbow macaroni	225 g	8 oz	½ lb
1 tbspn oil			

Trim the pork fillet and cut into slices about ½ inch/1 cm thick. Fry quickly in the butter until browned, then remove from the pan. Fry the mushrooms and onions until just turning colour then remove from heat and add the flour and tomato purée. Cook gently, stirring, and season with the sugar, salt and pepper. Blend in the soured cream and add the meat. If necessary, add a little stock or water so that the meat is covered. Simmer gently for 10 minutes or until the meat is tender.

Meanwhile boil the macaroni in a large saucepan of well-salted water for 14 minutes or until just cooked. Drain well and toss with the oil. Arrange the macaroni in a border round a hot serving dish, spoon the meat into the centre.

Spiced ham croquettes
Sliced fresh peaches with cream

Spiced ham croquettes

INGREDIENTS	METRIC	IMP.	U.S.
Milk	450 ml	$\frac{3}{4}$ pint	$1\frac{3}{4}$ cups
Fine semolina	100 g	4 oz	$\frac{3}{4}$ cup
Salt and pepper			
Cooked ham	175 g	6 oz	6 oz
Grated Gruyère cheese	75 g	3 oz	$\frac{3}{4}$ cup
Seasoned flour for coating			
Oil for frying			
2 tbspns grated onion			
1 clove garlic, chopped			
1 tbspn oil			
Tomatoes	225 g	8 oz	$\frac{1}{2}$ lb
Coarsely ground black pepper			
Sprigs of fresh herbs to garnish			

First make the croquettes. Bring the milk to the boil, sprinkle in the semolina, and cook, stirring, until thick and smooth. Season with salt and pepper to taste. Remove from the heat. Finely chop the ham and grate the cheese. Stir these into the sauce. Allow to get cold. Shape the mixture into small croquettes, coating them in seasoned flour. Deep fry in hot oil for about 3-4 minutes, until golden brown. (If it is necessary to shallow-fry the croquettes, turn carefully with a spatula to brown on all sides.) Meanwhile mix together the grated onion, chopped garlic and the oil. Halve the tomatoes, spread each half with a little of the onion mixture, sprinkle with salt and coarsely ground black pepper and place under a hot grill. Serve the croquettes and hot tomatoes, garnished with sprigs of herbs.

Curried fish kedgeree
Blackberry and apple coupes

Curried fish kedgeree

INGREDIENTS	METRIC	IMP.	U.S.
Cod fillet	350 g	12 oz	$\frac{3}{4}$ lb
Smoked cod fillet	225 g	8 oz	$\frac{1}{2}$ lb
1 tbspn oil			
Butter	50 g	2 oz	$\frac{1}{4}$ cup
1 large onion, chopped			
Long grain rice	100 g	4 oz	$\frac{1}{2}$ cup+
1 tbspn curry powder			
1 tspn salt			
Canned red pimientoes	150 g	5 oz	5 oz

Poach the white and smoked fish in gently boiling water until just tender. Drain, and flake. Heat the oil and butter and use to sauté the onion until pale golden, stir in the rice, curry powder and salt and cook, stirring, for 2 minutes. Add $\frac{1}{2}$ pint/ 300 ml/$1\frac{1}{4}$ cups boiling water, cover and cook until all the water is absorbed. Chop the pimiento, reserving the liquor. Add this to the rice mixture if it becomes too dry. Stir the pimiento into it with the flaked fish and heat through. Transfer to a warm serving dish and garnish with parsley.

Blackberry and apple coupes

INGREDIENTS	METRIC	IMP.	U.S.
1 packet apple sauce mix, or Sweet apple purée [applesauce]	300 ml	$\frac{1}{2}$ pint	$1\frac{1}{4}$ cups
Chopped toasted almonds or hazelnuts	25 g	1 oz	$\frac{1}{4}$ cup
Double [whipping] cream	150 ml	$\frac{1}{4}$ pint	$\frac{1}{2}$ cup
1 egg white			
Fresh blackberries or raspberries	450 g	1 lb	1 lb

Make up the sauce as directed on the packet. Stir in the nuts. Whip the cream, place a little in a piping bag for decoration and fold the remainder into the apple mixture. Whisk the egg white until stiff and fold into the apple cream. Arrange layers of blackberries and apple cream in glass dishes and decorate with whipped cream.

Courgette salad
Chicken and ham patties

Courgette salad

INGREDIENTS	METRIC	IMP.	U.S.
Courgettes [zucchini]	225 g	8 oz	$\frac{1}{2}$ lb
2 tspns lemon juice			
Button mushrooms	100 g	4 oz	1 cup
3 tbspns French [Italian] dressing			
Green salad			

Slice the courgettes thinly and blanch for 2 minutes in boiling salted water. Drain well and sprinkle with half the lemon juice. Slice the mushrooms thinly and toss in 2 tablespoons hot courgette water over moderate heat for 1 minute. Drain well and sprinkle with the remaining lemon juice. When completely cold, combine with the salad dressing and chill in a covered dish for at least 1 hour. Serve on a bed of green salad.

Chicken and ham patties

INGREDIENTS	METRIC	IMP.	U.S.
Chopped cooked chicken	175 g	6 oz	1 cup
Chopped cooked ham	100 g	4 oz	$\frac{2}{3}$ cup
Pinch of dried mixed herbs			
Butter	25 g	1 oz	2 tbspns
2 tbspns flour			
6 tbspns chicken stock [broth]			
Salt and pepper			
3 tbspns milk			
1 egg			
Puff pastry [paste]	225 g	8 oz	$\frac{1}{2}$ lb
Beaten egg			

Combine the chicken, ham and herbs. Melt the butter in a saucepan and stir in the flour. Cook gently for 2 minutes. Gradually add the stock and season to taste. Bring to boiling point, stirring. Cook for 4 minutes and stir in the milk. Remove from the heat and beat in the egg. Stir in the meat mixture, adjust the seasoning and leave to get cold. Meanwhile, roll out the pastry and cut out 8 large circles. Use half of these to line Yorkshire pudding (large muffin) tins. Fill with the chicken mixture and cover with the remaining pastry rounds. Moisten and seal the edges. Prick the tops, brush with beaten egg and bake in a hot oven (425°F, 220°C, Gas Mark 7) for 20-25 minutes, until golden brown.

MENU

24

Fried cod with beetroot and
horseradish cream
Fried potatoes
Pear and apricot whip

Fried cod with beetroot and horseradish cream

INGREDIENTS	METRIC	IMP.	U.S.
8 small cod fillets			
Oil for frying			
BATTER			
Self-raising flour [all-purpose flour + 2 tspns baking powder]	225 g	8 oz	2 cups
Pinch salt			
1 tbspn oil			
Warm water			
1 egg white			
SAUCE			
1 small canned red pimiento			
2 tbspns finely diced apple			
2 tbspns finely diced beetroot [beets]			
2 tbspns grated horseradish			
Whipped cream			
Salt and pepper			
1 lemon and 1 bunch parsley to garnish			

First make the batter. Put the flour and salt in a basin, make a well in the centre, pour in the oil and beat well, gradually drawing in the dry ingredients and adding sufficient warm water to give a smooth but fairly thick batter. Beat the egg white until stiff and fold into the batter. It improves if allowed to stand for a short while before using. To make the sauce, chop the pimiento very finely, fold in the apple, beetroot and horseradish and add sufficient cream to coat well. Season to taste and pile into a sauce boat. (A milder sauce can be made by decreasing the amount of horseradish and increasing the amount of beetroot and apple.) To cook the fish, dip the fillets into the batter and plunge straight into hot deep oil in a frying basket. Cook for 8-10 minutes, or until golden brown. Drain on absorbent kitchen paper and pile up on a warm serving dish. Garnish with knotted lemon halves and sprigs of parsley.

Pear and apricot whip

INGREDIENTS	METRIC	IMP.	U.S.
6 tbspns evaporated milk			
3 ripe pears			
Canned apricot halves	225 g	8 oz	8 oz
2 tbspns lemon juice			
Finely grated rind of 1 orange			
4 'finger' biscuits			
4 orange jelly slices			

Chill the evaporated milk. Peel and core the pears. Drain the apricots. Reserve a little fruit and liquidize or sieve the remainder with the lemon juice until smooth. Chop the reserved fruit and add to the purée. Whisk the evaporated milk until really thick and creamy, then fold in the fruit purée and orange rind. Spoon into 4 glasses and chill. Decorate each dessert with a finger biscuit and an orange jelly slice.

Sausages Somerset style
Cheddar cheese platter with celery hearts

Sausages Somerset style

INGREDIENTS	METRIC	IMP.	U.S.
Pork sausages [links]	450 g	1 lb	1 lb
Butter	15 g	$\frac{1}{2}$ oz	1 tbspn
Sliced onion	50 g	2 oz	$\frac{1}{4}$ cup
3 eating apples			
1 tspn crushed coriander seeds			
Cider	150 ml	$\frac{1}{4}$ pint	$\frac{1}{2}$ cup
Single cream [half & half]	50 ml	2 fl oz	$\frac{1}{4}$ cup
Salt and pepper			
2 slices white bread			
Bacon fat [dripping] or butter			

Fry the sausages in the butter until browned. Remove them from the pan and fry the sliced onion until lightly browned. Peel and slice the apples; add to the onions and fry until softened. Add the sausages, coriander seeds and cider. Cook gently for 10 minutes. Remove from the heat and stir in the cream. Season to taste with salt and pepper. Transfer to a warm serving dish. Remove the crusts from the bread and cut each slice into 4 triangles. Fry the bread triangles in the bacon dripping or butter until golden and crisp, turning once. Arrange the fried bread around the sausage mixture. Serve with buttered spring cabbage.

MENU

26

Stuffed courgettes with rice
Fresh pears with cream

Stuffed courgettes with rice

INGREDIENTS	METRIC	IMP.	U.S.
3 large courgettes [zucchini]			
Tomatoes	350 g	12 oz	$\frac{3}{4}$ lb
4 spring onions [scallions], chopped			
1 clove garlic, crushed			
2 tbspns oil			
Cooked sweetbreads	175 g	6 oz	$1\frac{1}{2}$ cups
Grated Gruyère [Swiss] cheese	50 g	2 oz	$\frac{1}{2}$ cup
1 tbspn flour			
Salt and pepper			
Long grain rice	100 g	4 oz	$\frac{1}{2}$ cup

Cut the courgettes in half lengthwise. Scoop out the flesh and cut into small dice. Chop the tomatoes and cook them with the courgette flesh, spring onion and garlic, until soft. Meanwhile oil a shallow ovenproof dish, arrange the courgette halves in it, sprinkle them with a few drops of oil and place in a moderately hot oven (375°F, 190°C, Gas Mark 5) for about 20 minutes, until the flesh begins to soften. Dice the sweetbreads and fold into the thick tomato mixture with the cheese and flour. Season to taste. Use the mixture to fill the courgette halves, return to the oven and cook for a further 20 minutes. Meanwhile, cook the rice in plenty of boiling salted water until tender. Drain and serve the courgettes on a bed of rice. Serves 3.

Fish duglère
Creamed potatoes
Blueberry pancake layer

Fish duglère

INGREDIENTS	METRIC	IMP.	U.S.
8 spring onions [scallions]			
2 cloves garlic			
Canned tomatoes	425 g	15 oz	15 oz
2 tbspns oil			
8 portions white fish fillet			
1 tspn salt			
$\frac{1}{4}$ tspn pepper			
2 tbspns chopped parsley			
Dry white wine	150 ml	$\frac{1}{4}$ pint	$\frac{1}{2}$ cup
1 tspn lemon juice			
Butter	15 g	$\frac{1}{2}$ oz	1 tbspn
Flour	15 g	$\frac{1}{2}$ oz	2 tbspns
Sprigs of parsley			

Chop the spring onions and crush the garlic. Drain the tomatoes, reserving the liquid, then chop the tomatoes. Place the garlic, onion and oil in a large frying pan. Season the fish with the salt and pepper, fold and arrange over the onion mixture. Spoon the tomato over the fish, sprinkle with the chopped parsley. Combine the wine and lemon juice and pour round the fish. Cut a circle of foil to fit the top of the pan and pierce the centre to let out steam. Place the foil lid lightly on the fish. Bring to boiling point, then cook gently for 10 minutes, or until the fish flakes easily when tested with a fork. Remove the portions of fish to warm serving dishes and keep hot. Melt the butter in a small pan, stir in the flour. Add the reserved liquid from the tomatoes and bring to boiling point, stirring constantly until the sauce is smooth and thick. Stir in the tomato mixture remaining in the frying pan. Adjust seasoning and spoon the sauce over the fish. Garnish with parsley sprigs. Serves 8.

Blueberry pancake layer

INGREDIENTS	METRIC	IMP.	U.S.
Plain [all-purpose] flour	100 g	4 oz	1 cup
¼ tspn salt			
2 eggs			
Milk	300 ml	½ pint	1¼ cups
1 tbspn melted fat [shortening]			
Canned blueberries	500 g	20 oz	2½ cups
1 tbspn cornflour [cornstarch]			
Rind and juice of 1 lemon			
Double [whipping] cream	300 ml	½ pint	1¼ cups

To make the pancakes, sieve the flour and salt into a bowl. Make a well in the centre and beat in the eggs and a little of the milk. Gradually beat in the remaining milk and the melted fat. Beat for 3-4 minutes. Lightly oil a frying pan. Use 2 tablespoons batter for each pancake, fry golden brown on both sides. Stack them on a tea towel. Continue to make the pancakes until the batter is finished. Drain the blueberries, reserving the syrup. Mix 2 tablespoons of the syrup with the cornflour and bring the remainder to the boil. Stir in the cornflour paste, lemon rind and juice. Cook and stir over low heat until thickened. Cool. Place a pancake on a serving dish. Whip the cream until stiff. Spread some over the pancake and scatter with some drained blueberries. Repeat until all the pancakes are used. Chill and serve in wedges. Hand the prepared blueberry sauce separately. Serves 8.
Note: If fresh blueberries are available, cook in water with sugar to sweeten until soft, and use juice as above.

61

MENU 28

Hot German potato salad
Green bean and frankfurter salad
Jambon aux fonds d'artichauts

Hot German potato salad

INGREDIENTS	METRIC	IMP.	U.S.
Cooked new potatoes	1 kg	2 lb	2 lb
Strong chicken stock [broth]	150 ml	¼ pint	½ cup +
Mayonnaise	150 ml	¼ pint	½ cup
2 tbspns chopped mixed fresh herbs (parsley, thyme, dill etc.)			
4 large gherkins			

Cook the potatoes in boiling salted water, drain and peel. Halve or quarter the potatoes while still warm, pour over the hot stock, then carefully fold in the mayonnaise and chopped herbs. Pile up in a serving dish or Tupperware Servalier bowl to keep hot. Serve warm, garnished with gherkin fans.

Note: To make gherkin fans, slice through lengthways about 6 times, almost to the base, and fan out.

Green bean and frankfurter salad

INGREDIENTS	METRIC	IMP.	U.S.
French [green] beans	350 g	12 oz	¾ lb
2 pairs frankfurter sausages			
4 tbspns French [Italian] dressing			

Cook the beans in boiling salted water then drain and reserve the cooking liquid. Keep the beans hot. Put the sausages in the hot liquid, bring almost to the boil, cover pan and allow to stand for 5 minutes, then drain and again reserve the liquid. Slice the sausages diagonally. Mix together the French dressing and 4 tablespoons of hot cooking liquid. Toss the hot beans and sliced sausage in this and turn into a serving dish or Tupperware Servalier bowl. Serve warm.

Hot German sausages, especially frankfurters and bratwurst make delicious main dishes combined with pasta, potatoes and other green vegetables, including sauerkraut. Canned sauerkraut often needs draining and rinsing to remove excessive saltiness so make a taste test. It is quite a delicacy when reheated with white wine and a small amount of oil to give it a gloss. You can also use lager or dry cider.

Jambon aux fonds d'artichauts

INGREDIENTS	METRIC	IMP.	U.S.
4 slices ham			
8 slices processed cheese			
2 hard-boiled eggs			
8 artichoke bottoms			
1 medium lettuce			
1 tbspn chopped parsley			
SAUCE			
Butter	25 g	1 oz	2 tbspns
Flour	25 g	1 oz	$\frac{1}{4}$ cup
Milk	185 ml	6 fl oz	$\frac{3}{4}$ cup
$\frac{1}{2}$ tspn French mustard			
Salt and pepper			

Divide the slices of ham in half and trim to the same size as the cheese slices. Shell the eggs, separate yolks from whites and push one yolk and one white separately through a coarse sieve. Roughly chop the remaining egg. To make the sauce, melt the butter, stir in the flour and cook for 2 minutes. Gradually add the milk and bring to the boil, stirring constantly. Add the mustard, season to taste with salt and pepper and stir in the chopped egg. Fill the artichoke bottoms with the egg mixture. Cover each with a slice of ham and a slice of cheese and grill until browned. Arrange a bed of lettuce on four serving plates. Place two grilled artichoke bottoms on each, and garnish with the sieved egg and chopped parsley.

MENU 29

Chicken livers in Madeira sauce
Tossed watercress salad
Chocolate orange dessert

Chicken livers in Madeira sauce

INGREDIENTS	METRIC	IMP.	U.S.
Long grain rice	150 g	5 oz	$\frac{3}{4}$ cup
1 tspn salt			
Chicken livers	350 g	12 oz	$\frac{3}{4}$ lb
Flour for coating			
1 apple			
Butter	40 g	$1\frac{1}{2}$ oz	3 tbspns
SAUCE			
Butter	25 g	1 oz	2 tbspns
Flour	25 g	1 oz	$\frac{1}{4}$ cup
Strong beef stock [broth]	450 ml	$\frac{3}{4}$ pint	2 cups
Madeira	4 tbspns	4 tbspns	$\frac{1}{3}$ cup

Cook the rice in $1\frac{3}{4}$ pints/1 litre/$4\frac{1}{2}$ cups boiling water with the salt for 12-15 minutes. Drain and keep hot. Meanwhile, make the sauce. Melt the butter, stir in the flour and cook, stirring, until golden brown. Gradually add the stock and bring to the boil, stirring constantly. Add the Madeira and cook for 5 minutes to reduce the sauce slightly. Coat the chicken livers lightly with flour and core and slice the apple. Melt the butter and use to fry the livers and apple slices for about 5 minutes, until livers are firm and just cooked through. Serve the livers with the hot rice and pour the sauce over. Garnish with apple slices. Serves 3.

Chocolate orange dessert

INGREDIENTS	METRIC	IMP.	U.S.
2 oranges			
Cream cheese	175 g	6 oz	6 oz
Icing [confectioner's] sugar	50 g	2 oz	$\frac{1}{2}$ cup
4 tbspns double [whipping] cream			
Seedless raisins	50 g	2 oz	$\frac{1}{2}$ cup
1 egg white			
Chocolate vermicelli [strands]			

Carefully peel and slice the oranges. Reserve the best slices for decoration. Place the remaining orange in the base of a serving dish. Cream the cheese, gradually beat in the sugar and cream. Stir in the raisins. Whisk the egg white until stiff and fold into the cheese mixture. Spoon over the orange in the dish, decorate with the reserved orange slices and chocolate vermicelli. Serves 3.

65

Raised game pie with Cran-apple relish
Red coleslaw with celery
Stilton cheese platter

Raised game pie

INGREDIENTS	METRIC	IMP.	U.S.
PASTRY			
Piain [all-purpose] flour	350 g	12 oz	3 cups
½ tspn salt			
Lard	100 g	4 oz	½ cup
Water	150 ml	¼ pint	½ cup + 2 tbspns
1 egg yolk			
FILLING			
1 pheasant or 2 partridges, boned			
Diced lean pork	225 g	8 oz	½ lb
Salt and pepper			
¼ tspn ground nutmeg			
Liquid aspic jelly [1 tbspn unflavored gelatin dissolved in 1¼ cups chicken broth]	300 ml	½ pint	

Sieve the flour and salt into a warm bowl, and rub in 1 oz/25 g of the fat. Place the remaining fat and water in a saucepan and heat until the fat melts. Pour into the flour with the egg yolk and beat with a wooden spoon until well blended. Knead the dough quickly on a lightly floured surface until it becomes a smooth round ball. Use the pastry while warm. Roll out two-thirds of the pastry and use to line a spring form raised pie mould. Cut the game into small pieces and layer in the pastry case with the pork, adding salt, pepper and nutmeg to each layer. Roll out remaining pastry to make a lid and seal the edges well together. Make a hole in the centre and decorate with pastry trimmings. Bake in a moderately hot oven (400°F, 200°C, Gas Mark 6) for 30 minutes then lower heat to moderate (350°F, 180°C, Gas Mark 4) for a further 2-2½ hours. Cover with greaseproof paper after 1 hour's cooking. Remove mould and cool pie. Pour in the liquid aspic jelly and allow to set. Serve cold with Cran-apple relish.

Hot water crust pastry can be used to make an elegant pie without a spring form mould. Shape two thirds of the pastry into a ball, flatten and place a jam jar in the centre. Put your clenched fist into the jam jar to hold it steady and use the other hand to press the pastry up round the sides. Work quickly before the pastry becomes too cold and set. Remove the jar, pack in the filling and use remaining pastry to make the lid. Always have some aspic or quick-setting stock ready to pour into the cooked pie when it is cool, through a hole in the lid.

Cran-apple relish

INGREDIENTS	METRIC	IMP.	U.S.
1 large cooking [baking] apple			
2 tbspns water			
1 tbspn soft [light] brown sugar			
½ tspn ground cloves			
Cranberries	225 g	8 oz	½ lb

Peel, core and slice the apple roughly into a small saucepan. Add the water and cook over low heat until reduced to a pulp, add the sugar, cloves and cranberries and continue cooking for a further few minutes until the cranberries burst. Stir well and cool. Serve with Raised game pie.

Red coleslaw with celery

INGREDIENTS	METRIC	IMP.	U.S.
1 small red cabbage			
3 large oranges			
½ head celery			
Walnut halves	50 g	2 oz	½ cup
Salt and pepper			
½ tspn mild continental mustard			
1 tbspn oil			

Shred the cabbage finely, removing the core and thick stems. Peel 2 of the oranges and divide into segments, discarding the pith and membrane. Chop the celery into short lengths and mix with the orange segments, cabbage and walnuts. Squeeze the juice from the remaining orange, season to taste with salt, pepper and mustard and beat in the oil. Use to toss the salad ingredients.

MENU

31

Hansel's curry soup
Glazed gammon with carrots
Buttered pasta shells
Sliced bananas with cream

Hansel's curry soup

INGREDIENTS	METRIC	IMP.	U.S.
Butter	25 g	1 oz	2 tbspns
1 small onion, chopped			
1 tbspn cornflour [cornstarch]			
1 tspn curry powder			
2 medium eating apples, peeled and diced			
Chicken stock [broth]	600 ml	1 pint	2½ cups
1 tbspn lemon juice			
Single cream [half & half]	150 ml	¼ pint	½ cup
1 red-skinned eating apple			
Sprig of watercress			

Melt the butter in a saucepan. Fry the onion in the melted butter until limp, but not brown. Stir in the cornflour and curry powder. Cook for 2-3 minutes. Add the diced apples, chicken stock and lemon juice. Cover and simmer for 30 minutes. Liquidise in a blender or sieve. Pour into a clean saucepan. Stir in the single cream and reheat gently. Core and chop the apple, and cut a few watercress leaves into strips. Serve the soup with the chopped apple and watercress garnish.

Glazed gammon with carrots

INGREDIENTS	METRIC	IMP.	U.S.
Joint corner gammon [ham butt]	1.5 kg	3 lb	3 lb
1 tspn ground cloves			
1 tbspn clear honey			
1 tbspn demerara [brown] sugar			
Carrots, sliced	450 g	1 lb	1 lb
Butter	15 g	½ oz	1 tbspn
1 medium onion, chopped			
Soured cream	150 ml	¼ pint	⅔ cup
Salt and pepper			

Soak the ham for several hours in cold water if very salty. (Ask the butcher as cured pork from different countries varies.) To cook, place the joint in a large pan, barely covered with fresh cold water and bring to the boil. Throw away the water, replace with fresh hot water, bring to the boil, lower heat and cover. Simmer for 30 minutes per pound/½ kg. Remove joint from pan and strip off skin. This is quite easy if the meat is cooked. Score the fat surface into 1 inch/2.5 cm squares. Mix together the honey and ground cloves and heat until melted. Use this mixture to brush over the fat surface of the joint, sprinkle with the sugar and place in a hot oven (425°F, 220°C, Gas Mark 7) for about 15 minutes, or until glaze is rich golden brown. If necessary, baste with the juices which come from the joint. Meanwhile, cook the carrots in boiling salted water until tender. Melt butter and use to fry the onion gently until limp. Stir in the cream and seasoning and heat through gently until hot. Pour over the cooked carrots and stir gently. Place the cooked joint on a hot serving dish and surround with the carrots.

68

MENU
32

Lamb with lemon herb stuffing
Maçedoine of vegetables and new potatoes
Pineapple ginger pudding with
Pineapple sauce

Lamb with lemon herb stuffing

INGREDIENTS	METRIC	IMP.	U.S.
1 boned shoulder of lamb			
STUFFING			
Sausagemeat [bulk pork sausage]	*225 g*	*8 oz*	*½ lb*
2 tbspns dry sage and onion stuffing mix			
½ tspn dried mixed herbs			
1 tbspn chopped chives			
Grated rind and juice of 1 lemon			
Salt and pepper			

First make the stuffing. Mix together the sausage meat, stuffing mix, herbs, chives, lemon juice and rind and seasoning. Spread on shoulder of lamb. Roll up the meat and tie securely. Roast in a moderate oven (350°F, 180°C, Gas Mark 4) for 40-45 minutes per pound/450 g. Serve with a maçedoine of spring vegetables and new potatoes. Serves 6.

Pineapple ginger pudding

INGREDIENTS	METRIC	IMP.	U.S.
Butter or margarine	100 g	4 oz	$\frac{1}{2}$ cup
Castor [granulated] sugar	100 g	4 oz	$\frac{1}{2}$ cup
2 large eggs			
Self-raising [all-purpose] flour	175 g	6 oz	$1\frac{1}{2}$ cups
Baking powder	1 tspn	1 tspn	$2\frac{1}{2}$ tspns
Pinch salt			
3 tbspns canned pineapple juice			
2 tbspns ginger marmalade			

Beat together the butter and sugar until light and fluffy. Gradually beat in the eggs and a little of the flour. Sieve the remaining flour with the baking powder and salt. Fold into the batter. Stir in 2 tablespoons pineapple juice. Grease a 2 pint/1 litre/5 cup pudding basin and spoon the ginger marmalade mixed with the remaining tablespoon of pineapple juice into the base. Fill the pudding basin with the batter and cover with greaseproof paper. Steam, tightly covered, for 2 hours. Turn out and serve with the pineapple sauce. Serves 6.

Pineapple sauce

INGREDIENTS	METRIC	IMP.	U.S.
2 tspns cornflour [cornstarch]			
Canned pineapple juice	300 ml	$\frac{1}{2}$ pint	$1\frac{1}{4}$ cups
Grated rind and juice of $\frac{1}{2}$ lemon			
1 tbspn butter			

Mix the cornflour with two tablespoons of the pineapple juice. Bring the remaining juice to the boil and stir in the cornflour paste. Stir in the lemon rind and juice. Cook and stir until thick and smooth, about 2-3 minutes. Beat in the butter. Serve over Pineapple ginger pudding.

Golden potato-topped pie with onions
Green peas
Beignets

Golden potato-topped pie with onions

INGREDIENTS	METRIC	IMP.	U.S.
2 beef stock [bouillon] cubes			
Minced [ground] cooked or raw lamb or beef	450 g	1 lb	1 lb
3 tbspns corn oil			
Finely chopped swede [rutabaga]	225 g	8 oz	1½ cups
1 tspn mixed sweet herbs			
1 tbspn tomato purée [paste]			
2 tspns brown sugar			
1 tbspn flour			
Salt and pepper			
Diced potatoes	450 g	1 lb	2 cups
Milk	150 ml	¼ pint	⅔ cup
1 egg			
4 medium onions			

Dissolve the stock cubes in 1 pint/½ litre/2½ cups boiling water. Sauté the meat in 2 tablespoons hot oil, stirring frequently, for 2 minutes. Add the swede, herbs, tomato purée, sugar, and finally the flour. Pour in half the stock and stir until thick over moderate heat. Taste and adjust seasoning. Cook the potatoes in boiling salted water, drain, mash with the milk, season well and beat in the egg. At the same time par-boil the onions in the remaining stock. Turn the meat mixture into a greased ovenproof dish, spread the mashed potato on top and fork up the surface. Arrange the onions in a small baking dish, mix the remaining corn oil with the rest of the stock and pour over them. Place both dishes in a hot oven (425°F, 220°C, Gas Mark 7) for 20 minutes, until golden.

Beignets

INGREDIENTS	METRIC	IMP.	U.S.
1 packet boudoir biscuits [ladyfingers], crushed			
Cream cheese	100 g	4 oz	4 oz
2 tbspns single cream [half & half]			
3 tbspns plain [all-purpose] flour			
2 eggs			
1 tbspn brandy or rum			
Oil for frying			
Castor [granulated] sugar for dredging			

Beat all the ingredients together and leave to stand for 15 minutes. Heat the oil until a piece of the paste begins to frizzle as soon as it is immersed in the oil. Form the mixture into pieces about the size of a walnut. Add a few at a time to the oil in a frying basket, cooking in batches. When golden brown remove carefully on to soft kitchen paper to drain. Keep warm until all the beignets are cooked. Serve dredged with castor sugar or with apricot jam.

73

Chicken with capers
Cauliflower florets
Chestnut soufflé
Coffee liqueur sauce

Chicken with capers

INGREDIENTS	METRIC	IMP	U.S.
Butter	75 g	3 oz	6 tbspns
Mushrooms, sliced	225 g	8 oz	2 cups
1 tbspn flour			
Milk	300 ml	½ pint	1¼ cups
Salt and pepper			
Juice of ½ lemon			
2 tbspns capers			
Cooked chicken, sliced	350 g	12 oz	¾ lb
2 hard-boiled eggs, quartered			
Paprika pepper			
Fried breat croûtons			

Melt the butter in a pan and use to sauté the mushrooms for 1 minute. Stir in the flour then gradually add the milk. Bring to the boil stirring constantly, and season to taste. Add the lemon juice and capers and cook for a further 5 minutes. Arrange the chicken slices and hard-boiled egg in a small ovenproof casserole and pour the sauce over. Cook in a moderately hot oven (375°F, 190°C, Gas Mark 5) for 10 minutes. Dust surface with paprika pepper and garnish with croûtons.

Chestnut soufflé

INGREDIENTS	METRIC	IMP.	U.S.
Chestnut purée	450 g	1 lb	1 lb
4 eggs, separated			
1 tbspn flour			
Few drops vanilla essence [extract]			

Butter an ovenproof soufflé dish. Beat the egg yolks into the chestnut purée, one at a time, sprinkling in a little flour with each addition. Beat the egg whites until stiff and fold lightly into the chestnut mixture with the vanilla essence. Pour into the prepared dish and bake in a moderately hot oven (375°F, 190°C, Gas Mark 5) for about 35 minutes, until well risen and golden brown. Serve at once with Coffee liqueur sauce.

Coffee liqueur sauce

INGREDIENTS	METRIC	IMP.	U.S.
Strong black coffee	300 ml	½ pint	1¼ cups
Pinch salt			
Sugar	50 g	2 oz	¼ cup
4 tbspns coffee liqueur			
2 tspns arrowroot			
1 egg yolk			
Knob of butter			

Heat the coffee, salt and sugar to boiling point and add the liqueur. Moisten the arrowroot with a little cold water, add to the pan and stir, over moderate heat, until the mixture clears. Remove sauce from heat, stir in the egg yolk quickly and then the butter to give the sauce a gloss.

MENU

35

Sausage and butter bean quickies
Orange 'n lemon beetroot
Frozen date and nut pie

Sausage and butter bean quickies

INGREDIENTS	METRIC	IMP.	U.S.
Sausages [links]	450 g	1 lb	1 lb
Canned butter beans	450 g	1 lb	1 lb
Milk	150 ml	¼ pint	½ cup
Butter	50 g	2 oz	¼ cup
1 large onion, sliced			
1 tbspn flour			
Salt and pepper			
Grated cheese	50 g	2 oz	½ cup
Chopped parsley			

Grill or fry the sausages until nicely brown all over. Strain the liquid from the beans and make up to ½ pint/300 ml with milk. Heat the butter in a saucepan and fry the onion gently until just coloured, remove from the heat and stir in the flour. Gradually blend in the liquid and bring to the boil, stirring constantly. Cook gently for 3 minutes. Mix in the butter beans, season to taste, and pour into a shallow ovenproof dish. Arrange the sausages on top and scatter the grated cheese over. Cook under the grill until golden and bubbling. Garnish with chopped parsley.

Orange 'n lemon beetroot

INGREDIENTS	METRIC	IMP.	U.S.
Fresh beetroot [beets]	*1 kg*	*2 lb*	*2 lb*
2 tbspns lemon juice			
Orange juice	*50 ml*	*2 fl oz*	*¼ cup*
1 tbspn wine vinegar			
1 tbspn clear honey			
1 tbspn cornflour [cornstarch]			
½ tspn salt			
Pinch pepper			
Butter	*50 g*	*2 oz*	*¼ cup*
½ tspn grated lemon rind			
½ tspn grated orange rind			

Cook the beetroot in boiling water until tender, about 50 minutes. Peel and cut into ½ inch/1 cm dice. Combine the lemon juice, orange juice, vinegar, honey and cornflour. Bring to the boil and cook over medium heat until the sauce is thick and clear. Remove from heat. Add the diced beetroot, salt, pepper and butter. Heat through. Pour into a serving dish and garnish with the grated orange and lemon rinds.

Frozen date and nut pie

INGREDIENTS	METRIC	IMP.	U.S.
8 digestive biscuits [12 graham crackers]			
Butter	*40 g*	*1½ oz*	*3 tbspns*
1 tbspn castor [granulated] sugar			
Vanilla ice cream	*600 ml*	*1 pint*	*2½ cups*
Chopped dates	*100 g*	*4 oz*	*⅔ cup*
Water	*75 ml*	*3 fl oz*	*⅓ cup*
1 tbspn granulated sugar			
2 tspns lemon juice			
Double [whipping] cream	*150 ml*	*¼ pint*	*½ cup*
2 tbspns castor [granulated] sugar			
½ tspn vanilla essence [extract]			
Chopped walnuts	*25 g*	*1 oz*	*¼ cup*

Crush the digestive biscuits. Melt the butter and stir into the crumbs with the castor sugar. Press into an 8 inch/20 cm pie dish and bake in a moderate oven (350°F, 180°C, Gas Mark 4) for 5 minutes. Cool. Stir the ice cream to soften and spoon into the biscuit crust. Place in the freezer. Combine the dates, water and sugar in a small saucepan. Cover and cook for 5 minutes or until soft. Stir in the lemon juice and let cool. Spread half the date mixture over the ice cream. Whisk the cream lightly: fold in the castor sugar, vanilla essence, chopped walnuts and remaining date mixture. Spread over the date mixture in the biscuit crust. Freeze. Serve chilled.

Nutty pork crescents
Tomato glazed chicory
Chilled pineapple poll

Nutty pork crescents

INGREDIENTS	METRIC	IMP.	U.S.
Pork sausagemeat [bulk pork sausage]	225 g	8 oz	$\frac{1}{2}$ lb
6 dates, stoned			
Chopped nuts	50 g	2 oz	$\frac{1}{2}$ cup
Salt and pepper			
Good pinch ground nutmeg			
1 egg, separated			
Puff pastry [paste]	350 g	12 oz	$\frac{3}{4}$ lb

Mix the sausagemeat with the finely chopped dates and the nuts, season well, bind with the lightly beaten egg white. Form into 8 sausage shapes with lightly floured hands. Roll out the pastry thinly, and cut into 8 squares. Place one piece of sausagemeat diagonally across the corner of a pastry square, roll across and fold in the other corners. Form into a crescent shape. Beat up the egg yolk with 2 tablespoons water and use to seal the parcel, turn over and brush with more egg wash. Make up the other seven parcels in the same way. Bake on a damped baking sheet in a hot oven (425°F, 220°C, Gas Mark 7) for 30 minutes.

Tomato glazed chicory

INGREDIENTS	METRIC	IMP.	U.S.
Heads of chicory [Belgian Endive]	450 g	1 lb	1 lb
Canned tomatoes	425 g	15 oz	15 oz
Few drops Tabasco			
1 tbspn clear honey			

Cook the chicory heads in boiling salted water until tender. Drain well and place in an oven-proof dish. Chop the tomatoes and stir in a few drops of Tabasco. Pour over the chicory in the dish and trickle over the honey. Place in a hot oven (220°C, 425°F, Gas Mark 7), for about 15 minutes until glazed.

Chilled pineapple poll

INGREDIENTS	METRIC	IMP.	U.S.
Canned pineapple slices	425 g	15 oz	15 oz
1 pineapple jelly [package pineapple flavored gelatin]			
Can creamed rice	430 g	15½ oz	15½ oz
Double [whipping] cream	150 ml	¼ pint	⅔ cup
Angelica to decorate			

Strain the syrup from the pineapple into a medium sized saucepan. Reserve 4 pineapple rings and chop the remainder. Break up the jelly, add to the syrup and heat gently to dissolve. Stir in the creamed rice and chopped pineapple. Divide the mixture between 4 individual dishes. Leave in a cool place until set. Whisk the cream until stiff and place in a piping bag. Put a slice of pineapple on top of each dessert. Pipe with large rosettes of cream and decorate with angelica 'leaves'. Served chilled.

Veal birds
Golden grapefruit sponge with
Grapefruit sauce

Veal birds

INGREDIENTS	METRIC	IMP.	U.S.
4 large or 8 small veal escalopes			
Butter	50 g	2 oz	$\frac{1}{4}$ cup
1 medium onion, chopped			
2 tbspns flour			
1 chicken stock [bouillon] cube			
Boiling water	450 ml	$\frac{3}{4}$ pint	2 cups
1$\frac{1}{2}$ tspns tomato purée [paste]			
1 bay leaf			
Salt and pepper			
Creamed potato	750 g	1$\frac{1}{2}$ lb	1$\frac{1}{2}$ lb
STUFFING			
Rolled oats	50 g	2 oz	$\frac{2}{3}$ cup
1 tbspn shredded [chopped beef] suet			
1 small onion, chopped			
1$\frac{1}{2}$ tspns chopped parsley			
1$\frac{1}{2}$ tspns chopped capers			
Grated rind of 1 lemon			
Salt and pepper			
1 egg, beaten			

First make the stuffing. Mix together all the ingredients then bind with the beaten egg. Flatten the escalopes slightly, trim and divide in half lengthwise if large. Place equal quantities of the stuffing at one end of each piece, roll up and tie with thread to form 'birds'. Melt the butter and use to fry the 'birds' until well browned. Remove and fry the onion lightly. Add the flour, fry for a few seconds, then gradually add the stock cube dissolved in the boiling water. Bring to the boil, stirring constantly. Add the tomato purée, bay leaf and seasoning and replace the 'birds'.

Reduce the heat, cover tightly and simmer for 45 minutes to 1 hour, or until the meat is tender. Remove threads and place 'birds' on a hot serving dish. Remove the bay leaf and pour the sauce over. Pipe a border of creamed potato round the outside of the dish.

Golden grapefruit sponge

INGREDIENTS	METRIC	IMP.	U.S.
Self-raising flour [all-purpose flour + 1¼ tspns baking powder]	150 g	5 oz	1¼ cups
Pinch of salt			
Butter	75 g	3 oz	6 tbspns
Castor [granulated] sugar	100 g	4 oz	½ cup
2 eggs, beaten			
1 tbspn milk			
Grated rind of ½ grapefruit			

Sieve the flour and salt together. In a separate bowl cream the butter and sugar until light and fluffy. Gradually add the eggs, alternately with the flour. Beat in the milk and grapefruit rind. Pour the mixture into a greased pudding basin and cover with foil. Steam for 1½ hours, turn out and serve with Grapefruit sauce.

Grapefruit sauce

INGREDIENTS	METRIC	IMP.	U.S.
2 grapefruit			
2-4 tbspns golden [corn] syrup			
1 tspn arrowroot			
Knob of butter			

Thinly pare the rind of one grapefruit and squeeze the juice from both. Place in a saucepan with golden syrup to taste and bring to the boil. Moisten the arrowroot with 2 tablespoons cold water, add to the pan and bring to the boil, stirring constantly until sauce clears. Beat in the butter and serve with Golden grapefruit sponge.

Fish pie with swede purée
Baked apples with maple syrup

Fish pie with swede purée

INGREDIENTS	METRIC	IMP.	U.S.
Cooked potato	450 g	1 lb	1 lb
Salt and pepper			
Little milk			
Cod fillet	450 g	1 lb	1 lb
Frozen peas	100 g	4 oz	1 cup
CHEESE SAUCE			
Milk	600 ml	1 pint	2½ cups
Butter	25 g	1 oz	2 tbspns
Flour	20 g	¾ oz	3 tbspns
Grated Cheddar cheese	100 g	4 oz	1 cup
SWEDE [RUTABAGA] PURÉE			
1 large or 2 medium swedes [rutabagas]			
Butter	25 g	1 oz	2 tbspns
½ tspn grated nutmeg			
Salt and pepper			
1 tbspn chopped parsley			

Mash the potato in the saucepan in which it was cooked, with seasoning to taste and sufficient milk to give a firm piping consistency. Keep hot. Poach the fish in the milk for the sauce and add seasoning to taste. Remove fish and flake roughly. To make the sauce, melt the butter in a saucepan and stir in the flour. Cook for 1 minute, stirring. Gradually add the strained milk from cooking the fish and bring to the boil, stirring constantly, until the sauce is smooth and thickened. Add the peas and grated cheese and reheat until bubbling. Lightly fold in the flaked fish and pour the mixture into a warm ovenproof glass dish. Place the warm potato in a piping bag fitted with a large star nozzle. Pipe large potato rosettes on the fish mixture to come well above the edge of the dish. Place under a moderately hot grill for a few minutes until the surface turns golden brown. Meanwhile, peel, chop and cook the swede until tender in boiling salted water. Drain well and mash with half the butter, the nutmeg, salt and pepper to taste. Turn purée into a warm serving dish, place the remaining butter in the centre and sprinkle with parsley. Serve with the hot fish pie.

MENU

39

Braised beef with mustard
Baked potatoes
Mincemeat cobbler

Braised beef with mustard

INGREDIENTS	METRIC	IMP.	U.S.
2 tspns dry mustard			
2 tbspns vinegar			
3 tbspns tomato purée [paste]			
2 tbspns corn oil			
1 small onion, chopped			
2 tbspns brown sugar			
1 tspn dried mixed herbs			
Salt and pepper			
Dripping	15 g	½ oz	1 tbspn
Joint silverside or brisket [boneless beef brisket]	1.5 kg	3 lb	3 lb
3 large onions, quartered			
3 large carrots, quartered			
2 tspns cornflour [cornstarch]			

Mix together the mustard and vinegar. Add the tomato purée, oil, onion, sugar, herbs and seasoning to taste and blend well together to make a sauce. Heat the dripping in a heavy saucepan and use to brown the joint all over. Add the onions and carrots round the joint and pour sauce over the meat. Cover with a close-fitting lid and simmer gently for 2½-3 hours, until the meat is tender. Remove joint to a warm serving dish, surround with the vegetables and keep hot. Moisten the cornflour with a little cold water and use to thicken the pan juices. Cook for 2 minutes, stirring constantly, and strain over the meat.

Mincemeat cobbler

INGREDIENTS	METRIC	IMP.	U.S.
8 small slices white bread			
Shredded [finely chopped] suet	75 g	3 oz	½ cup
Demerara or soft [light] brown sugar	75 g	3 oz	6 tbspns
1 tspn ground cinnamon			
Cooking [winter] pears	450 g	1 lb	1 lb
Grated rind and juice of 1 lemon			
Mincemeat	225 g	8 oz	1 cup

Using a 2½ inch/6 cm cutter, cut out 7 rounds from 7 slices of the bread. Make breadcrumbs from leftover slice and pieces of bread. Mix together suet, sugar and cinnamon. Combine the breadcrumbs with two-thirds of the suet mixture. Sprinkle one half over the base of a greased 1½-2 pint/1 litre round ovenproof dish. Bake in a moderately hot oven (400°F, 200°C, Gas Mark 6) for 10 minutes. Peel, core and grate pears. Combine with the lemon rind and juice, and the mincemeat. Spread half the fruit mixture over the crumb base and cover with remaining breadcrumbs, then the remaining fruit mixture. Arrange rounds of bread overlapping slightly on top leaving a round of fruit mixture showing in the centre. Sprinkle remaining third of suet, sugar and cinnamon mixture over the bread and bake for 20-25 minutes until top is crisp and golden.

MENU 40

Brunch kidneys
Scrambled eggs with crumbled crispy bacon
Poppy seed plait
Hungarian bubble loaf
Almond apricot conserve

Brunch kidneys

INGREDIENTS	METRIC	IMP.	U.S.
6 lambs' kidneys			
Pork chipolata sausages (small pork links)	450 g	1 lb	1 lb
Butter	50 g	2 oz	$\frac{1}{4}$ cup
4 tbspns cornflour [cornstarch]			
Beef stock [broth]	450 ml	$\frac{3}{4}$ pint	2 cups
1 tbspn Worcestershire sauce			
2 tspns mild mustard			
1 tbspn vinegar			
1 tbspn brown sugar			
Salt and pepper			
Button mushrooms	225 g	8 oz	$\frac{1}{2}$ lb
6 hard-boiled eggs			
Chopped parsley			

Skin, halve and core the kidneys. Fry the kidneys and sausages gently in the butter until sealed and brown on all sides. Blend the cornflour with the stock, and add the Worcestershire sauce, mustard, vinegar, and sugar. Season to taste. Pour over the sausage mixture and bring to boiling point, stirring constantly. Simmer for 5 minutes. Add the mushrooms and cook for a further 5 minutes. Halve the hard-boiled eggs, add to the pan and heat through gently. Garnish with chopped parsley. Serves 12.

Enriched white bread

INGREDIENTS	METRIC	IMP.	U.S.
Dried yeast or	25 g	1 oz	$2\frac{1}{2}$ tbspns
Fresh [compressed] yeast	50 g	2 oz	1 cake
Warm water	150 ml	$\frac{1}{4}$ pint	$\frac{2}{3}$ cup
Strong plain [all-purpose] flour	1.5 kg	3 lb	12 cups
Milk	450 ml	$\frac{3}{4}$ pint	2 cups
Margarine	150 g	5 oz	$\frac{2}{3}$ cup
2 tspns malt extract			
1 tbspn salt			
2 eggs			

Dissolve the yeast in the warm water and beat in 8 oz/225 g flour. Cover with a damp cloth and let rise for 30 minutes. Scald the milk; add the margarine, malt and salt. Cool to lukewarm. Beat the eggs lightly and add to the sponge. Then beat in the scalded milk mixture and the remaining flour. Mix with the hand until it forms a soft, but not sticky dough. Cover with a damp cloth and let rise in a warm place until doubled in bulk, about 1 hour. Divide the dough into two.

Poppy seed plait: You will require one beaten egg to glaze and 2 tablespoons poppy seed. On a floured board, roll one piece of the dough into three long strips. Plait the three strips of dough together on a greased baking tray. Let double in bulk. Brush with beaten egg and sprinkle with poppy seeds. Bake in a hot oven (425°F, 220°C, Gas Mark 7) for 10 minutes, then lower heat to moderately hot (400°F, 200°C, Gas Mark 6) for 25 minutes. Cool on a wire rack.

Brunch for 12 people
Make the bread the previous
day and refrigerate overnight,
and lay the table ready for
the Brunch. In the morning,
set out baskets of sliced
bread, dishes of butter,
Almond apricot conserve and
jugs of milk or cream.
Prepare the Brunch kidneys
and fry the bacon very crisp.
Drain the bacon on soft
kitchen paper, crumble and
spoon over the scrambled
eggs which should be
cooked last of all when
coffee and tea are brewed
and piping hot. (Allow 1
slice bacon and at least 1
scrambled egg per person.)

Hungarian bubble loaf Roll the other piece of
dough into small balls. Melt 100 g/4 oz/½ cup butter.
Roll the balls in the butter then in a mixture of 50 g/
2 oz/¼ cup brown sugar and 2 teaspoons ground
cinnamon. Place a layer of coated balls in a buttered
9 inch/23 cm ring cake tin. Scatter a few chopped
nuts and glacé (candied) cherries on top. Alternate
layers of coated dough balls, nuts and cherries until
half the tin is filled. Cover and let rise in a warm place
until dough reaches top of tin. Bake as for Poppy seed
plait until golden brown.

Almond apricot conserve

INGREDIENTS	METRIC	IMP.	U.S.
2 large oranges			
Apricots	1.25 kg	3 lb	3 lb
Ground almonds	50 g	2 oz	2 oz
Sugar	1.25 kg	3 lb	6 cups

Peel the rind from the oranges thinly, cut them in
half and spoon out the flesh. Roughly chop the
rind. Cover with water, bring to the boil and cook
for 4 minutes. Strain off the water, add the softened rind to the halved and stoned apricots. (If
large, quarter the apricots.) Put the orange flesh,
rind and apricots in a preserving pan and cook
gently until the apricots are soft. Add the ground
almonds and sugar and bring back to the boil.
Cook rapidly until the conserve sets when tested.

MENU

41

Basting sauce
Lamburgers
Kebabs
Potato and bacon salad
Red and white coleslaw

Basting sauce:
Combine 1 teaspoon each mild chilli powder and celery salt, 2 tablespoons each of brown sugar and Worcestershire sauce and 3 tablespoons tomato ketchup (catsup). Dilute this mixture with 150 ml/¼ pint/½ cup beef stock (broth) and add a few drops of Tabasco. Heat until the sugar dissolves and use to brush lamburgers, kebabs, etc. during cooking.

Lamburgers:
Finely chop 1 small onion and fry gently in 25 g/1 oz/2 tablespoons butter until soft. Mix with 450 g/1 lb minced (ground) lamb, 1 finely chopped stick of celery, 2 table-spoons tomato purée (paste), 1 teaspoon dried mixed herbs, 50 g/2 oz/⅔ cup fresh white breadcrumbs and salt and pepper to taste. Divide into 12 equal portions and shape each into a round flat cake. Barbecue the burgers for about 15 minutes, until golden brown on both sides, brushing occasionally with the sauce.

Kebabs:
Thread skewers with a selection of pieces of diced lamb, quartered tomatoes and small onions and button mush-rooms. Brush with the basting sauce and barbecue for about 15 minutes, until the lamb is well cooked.

Potato and bacon salad:
Dice 450 g/1 lb freshly boiled and skinned potatoes and combine while still warm with 4 tablespoons chicken stock (broth). Crisply fry 4 rashers (slices) bacon, cut into small pieces and stir into the potato mixture with 4 tablespoons mayonnaise. Season to taste.

Barbecue supper for 12 people
To serve everyone comfortably, allow one lamburger, one kebab, and one chop or piece of lamb fillet per person. As well as the selection of salads, serve bran rolls or miniature wholemeal loaves with butter. Don't forget a basket of polished red dessert apples and plenty of hot coffee.

Red and white coleslaw:
Finely slice 100 g/4 oz/1 cup each red and white cabbage. Beat together 2 tablespoons natural (plain) yogurt with 2 tablespoons oil-and-vinegar dressing, pour over the cab-bage and chill for at least 1 hour.

86

MENU

42

Melon with Parma ham
Italian supper dish
Sorrento salad
Gorgonzola cheese with peaches

Melon with Parma ham

INGREDIENTS	METRIC	IMP.	U.S.
1 small honeydew melon			
4 slices fresh Parma ham			

Chill the whole melon for at least one hour before needed. Cut the melon into four equal slices. Spoon out the seeds and run a shaped grape fruit knife along the flesh close to the rind. Wrap a slice of Parma ham round each piece of melon and serve.

Italian supper dish

INGREDIENTS	METRIC	IMP.	U.S.
Wholewheat spaghetti rings	350 g	12 oz	$\frac{3}{4}$ lb
Pork sausagemeat [bulk pork sausage]	450 g	1 lb	1 lb
2 tspns Worcestershire sauce			
Garlic salt and pepper			
Oil for frying			
2 medium onions			
Canned tomatoes	425 g	15 oz	15 oz
Butter	25 g	1 oz	2 tbspns
Sliced button mushrooms	50 g	2 oz	$\frac{3}{4}$ cup
Flour	25 g	1 oz	$\frac{1}{4}$ cup
1 tspn dried mixed herbs			

Cook the pasta in plenty of boiling salted water for 12 minutes, or until tender. Meanwhile, combine the sausagemeat, Worcestershire sauce, garlic salt and pepper to taste. Shape into 16 small balls and shallow fry in a little oil for about 6 minutes, until golden brown all over, turning frequently. Drain well and keep hot. Chop the onions and tomatoes. In a clean pan, melt the butter and use to fry the onion until soft. Add the mushrooms and cook for a further 2 minutes. Stir in the flour and cook for 1 minute. Add the tomatoes and liquid from the can and the herbs and bring to the boil, stirring constantly. Simmer for 5 minutes. Drain the spaghetti rings and place in a warm serving dish. Top with the sausage balls and coat with some of the tomato sauce. Hand the rest of the sauce separately.

Sorrento salad

INGREDIENTS	METRIC	IMP.	U.S.
Canned anchovy fillets	50 g	2 oz	2 oz
2 tspns lemon juice			
Black pepper			
Small cauliflower florets	225 g	8 oz	1 cup
1 small dill pickle			
1 tbspn drained capers			
2 hard-boiled eggs			

Drain the oil from the anchovies into a small basin and beat in the lemon juice and black pepper to taste. Place the florets in a salad bowl, pour over the dressing and toss well. Cover and allow to stand for at least 2 hours. Thinly slice pickle, add to bowl with anchovies and capers. Quarter the eggs and use to garnish the salad.

Adding inspiration to cheese

The new approach to menu planning limits the number of courses to two except for formal occasions. Since so many people have to keep an eye on their weight, puddings and desserts are not always a popular choice for the second course. Cheese, which partners fresh fruit perfectly, is a wise choice and allows various members of the family to take large or small helpings as they wish. Also, when preparation time is limited, it is both quick and easy to arrange.

Simple cheese board: Even among our own home-produced cheeses there is a wide selection. Of the hard varieties – Cheddar, Double Gloucester, Caerphilly, Lancashire, White and Red Leicester, White and Blue Stilton, White, Red and Blue Cheshire, to name only those readily available. To lend added interest to the board, include Sage Derby, prettily streaked with green, and Red Windsor with wine red. We are not renowned for cream and curd cheeses from special districts but you can buy full fat cream cheeses, curd cheese and cottage cheese by weight. An interesting cheese board would include one classic hard cheese, one more exotic of the same type and a soft cheese for those who like a spreading texture.

Making a cheese platter: This is really a tray comprising all the items needed for the cheese course. A selection of breads, crispbreads and biscuits of the cracker type look well if arranged together in a small basket lined with a clean napkin. A small dish of butter which is soft enough to spread easily will find a place on the platter unless you always put a butter dish on the table. To complete the platter, add a touch of colour and flavour contrast with one of the following extras. Crisp, chilled celery, radishes or mild spring onions suit many tastes. Dishes of pickled onions, piccalilli or pickled walnuts are often enjoyed. Cutting out the sweet course will be no deprivation if the platter is made up with ripe fresh fruit. Apples and pears are particularly good with cheese. Grapes, plums, greengages, satsumas and clementines seem to complement the flavour of hard cheeses, while fresh pineapple is delicious with a soft creamy cheese. A dish of chopped fresh herbs, including chives, would make up an unusual and successful platter with a choice of soft cheeses. If you have a pepper mill with black peppercorns, so much the better.

Choosing foreign cheeses: Most people have their favourite cheeses from abroad, particularly French and Italian. The popular French soft cheeses, Camembert, Brie, Coulommiers, Pont l'Evêque and Carré de l'Est must be ripe but not overmature. It requires experience to judge these cheeses correctly in the shop, especially if they are kept chilled and it often pays to buy them only from a trusted supplier. If there is any doubt, go for the flavoured cream cheeses of the Boursin type, or semi-hard French cheeses such as Port Salut and Tome de Savoie. (The latter looks so pretty enclosed in its brownish-purple crust of dried grape pips.) These are not so delicate and are likely to stay in perfect condition for more than just a few days. Roquefort and Bleu de Bresse are strong French blue cheeses which rapidly become too pungent so do not expect them to store well. Although there are not so many Italian cheeses to choose from, they do cover the range of soft and hard varieties. Parmesan is very hard indeed and not really meant for the cheese board; Gorgonzola is a magnificent semi-hard blue cheese; Bel Paese is a much milder one and there are soft cheeses such as Mozzarella and Ricotta (lovely for salads). Dutch Gouda and Edam are excellent table cheeses and the red waxy overcoat gives Edam its special attraction.

Exotic touches: In some countries cheeses are offered with decorative touches you might like to copy. The Danish version of Camembert usually appears with a crown of overlapping orange or mandarin segments round the top. Soft cheeses in France are arranged on straw mats or on a bed of fresh green vine leaves. As well as wedges, or small whole cheeses, you could include potted cheese in the selection. Here is an easy way to make it at home.

Potted Lancashire cheese: Grate or crumble 450g/1 lb of very fresh Lancashire cheese. Put it in a pan together with 7 tablespoons of dry sherry and an equal quantity of lightly whipped cream. Season with salt and pepper to taste and place over gentle heat, stirring constantly, until the cheese melts. If liked, stir in some very finely chopped herbs such as parsley or chives. When the mixture is smooth, pour into small pots. Cool and cover the surface of each pot with a thin layer of melted butter. Store in the refrigerator and use up within one month.

Storing cheeses successfully: Do not expose the cut surfaces of cheese to the air longer than is necessary. Soft cheeses tend to ooze and run, hard cheeses tend to dry up and form an oily crust. All cheeses are best stored wrapped, using cling wrap to press close to the surface, and not necessarily in the refrigerator if there is a cool shelf as an alternative. Refrigerated and frozen cheeses need to return slowly to room temperature to develop full flavour and natural texture.

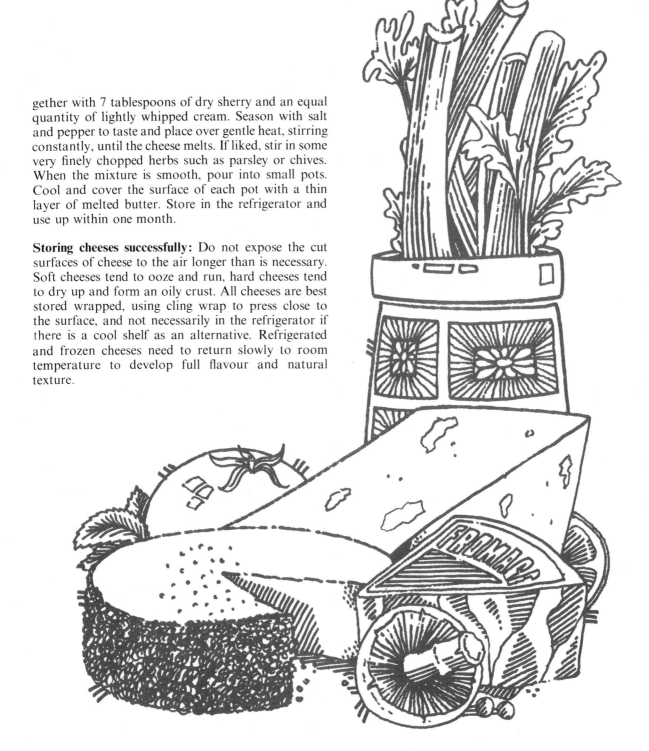

Acknowledgments
The author and publishers thank the following for their help
in supplying photographs for this book, some of which
were adapted from Four Seasons Cookery:
John Lee Studio
Roy Rich, Angel Studio
Christian Delu
Olives From Spain, p. 18-19, p. 44-45
The U.S. Rice Council, p. 24-25, p. 64-65
Buxted Brand Products by Ross Poultry Limited, p. 26-27
John West Foods Ltd, p. 26-27, p. 70-71
Culpeper Herbs and Spices, p. 28-29
Tower Housewares Ltd., p. 32-33
Atora – R.H.M. Foods Ltd., p. 36-37
New Zealand Lamb Information Bureau, p. 40-41, p. 70-71,
    p. 86-87
California Wine Institute, p. 46-47, p. 60-61
Trex, p. 48-49
The National Dairy Council, p. 48-49
The Apple and Pear Development Council, p. 50-51
The Pasta Information Bureau, p. 52-53
Buxted Advisory Service, p. 54-55
Knorr, p. 54-55, p. 72-73
The British Sausage Bureau, p. 58-59, p. 76-77, p. 84-85
The Tupperware Co. Ltd., p. 62-63
Hassy Perfection Celery, p. 66-67
Ambrosia Creamed Rice, p. 78-79
Quaker Oats, p. 80-81
Pasta Foods Ltd., p. 88-89

Lunch and Supper MENUS

Index

Almond apricot conserve   85
Apple snow   20
Apricot ice cream   16
Artichoke omelette   36
Aubergines in cream cheese   34

Basting sauce   86
Beef and egg pies   48
Beef stew with apricot dumplings   38
Beignets   73
Blackberry and apple coupes   54
Blackberry and pear pudding   42
Blueberry pancake layer   61
Braised beef with mustard   83
Brunch kidneys   84

Caramel snow eggs   23
Cheesey Charlies with spiced cherry
   sauce   37
Chestnut soufflé   74
Chicken and ham patties   55
Chicken and chips in a basket   30
Chicken livers in Madeira sauce   64
Chicken liver terrine   16
Chicken with capers   74
Chilled pineapple poll   79
Chocolate orange dessert   65
Cider and sultana sponge pudding   25
Coffee and nut ice cream   46
Coffee liqueur sauce   74
Courgette salad   55
Courgettes with black olives   51
Cran-apple relish   67
Creamy vegetable casserole   19
Crisp celery salad   33
Curried fish kedgeree   54

Enriched white bread   84

Fish duglère   60
Fish in capered mayonnaise   46
Fish pie with swede purée   82
Flaky pastry   41
Fried cod with beetroot and horseradish
   cream   56
Frozen date and nut pie   77

Glazed gammon with carrots   68
Golden grapefruit sponge   81
Golden potato-topped pie with onions
   72
Gooseberry fool with ice cream   29
Grape and coconut flan   39

Grapefruit sauce   81
Green bean and frankfurter salad   62
Greengage strudel   41

Hansel's curry soup   68
Herring potato balls with dill   34
Hot German potato salad   62
Hungarian bubble loaf   85

Italian supper dish   88

Jambon aux fonds d'artichauts   63

Kebabs   86

Lamburgers   86
Lamb with lemon herb stuffing   70
Loganberry ice cream   34

Mackerel with apple stuffing   50
Mincemeat cobbler   83

Nutty pork crescents   78

Orange and apricot sauce   22
Orange-basted chicken with baby
   beetroots   22
Orange hollandaise sauce   29
Orange 'n lemon beetroot   77
Orange sorbet shells   19
Oysters with croquettes   32

Pancake soufflé   51
Pan chicken and vegetables   46
Pasta with pork stroganoff   52
Peach toasts   45
Pear and apricot whip   57
Pineapple ginger pudding   71
Pineapple sauce   71
Plum flan with raisin sauce   31
Poppy seed plait   84
Potato and bacon salad   86
Prawn and olive starter   18

Quick scalloped cauliflower   22

Raised game pie   66
Red and white coleslaw   86
Red coleslaw with celery   67
Rhubarb and mandarin tart   27
Rhubarb and orange fool with cinnamon
   fingers   36

Roast lamb with lemon chutney
   sauce   40

Salade aux chapons   25
Sausage and butterbean quickies   76
Sausages Somerset style   58
Scallop mélange au gratin   42
Sole with spiced butter   28
Sorrel-stuffed eggs   20
Sorrento salad   88
Southern fried chicken with concasse
   of tomatoes   26
Spanish tortilla omelette   44
Spiced ham croquettes   53
Spiced cherry sauce   37
Stuffed courgettes with rice   59

Tomato glazed chicory   79
Tourte au chou   20
Turkey and apricot pilau   25

Veal birds   80
Vicarage trifle   49

Zabaglione   33

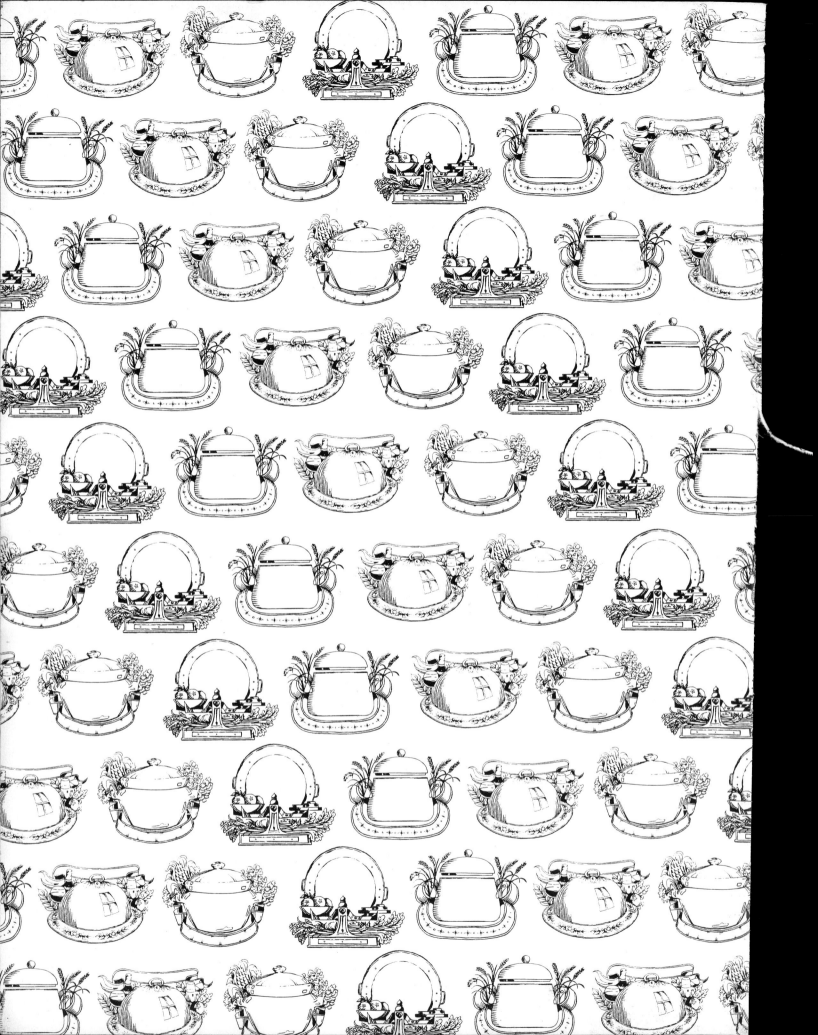